Sandra's Legacy

Frozen In Time

Roberta W. Quam

Published by Wendy Quammen DBA R W Quam

QUAMMEN, WENDY DBA QUAM, ROBERTA W, Author

SANDRA'S LEGACY: FROZEN IN TIME

WENDY QUAMMEN DBA R W QUAM

sandralegacy.com

This book is dedicated to the memory of:

My loving mother, Dorothy,

My father, Irvin, (The Professor) and

My sister, Donna, who passed away at the tender age of sixteen

on a cold winter day in January, 1964

It's January, 1964 and Sandra Chaudry is a lonely girl whose mother passed away when she was only five. Now seventeen, she's about to begin one of the most pivotal years of her life. Sandra's father, Professor of Anthropology at Harvard, is her closest friend. But then, her father gives her some disturbing news that changes Sandra's life forever—he must go far away for many months. Sandra's creepy and seemingly detached, coldhearted Aunt will be taking his place while he is gone.

During Sandra's time without her father she experiences her first love. Mysterious family secrets unfold. Sandra experiences supernatural encounters and she embarks on thrilling travel adventures. Sandra discovers the power of faith and ultimately rekindles a true and everlasting connection with her mother.

Travel back in time to 1964 and join Sandra on her fantastical journey, as she transforms from a solitary girl who misses her dear mother every day to a strong young woman who leaves a legacy for future generations.

PROLOGUE

Sandra Chaudhary lived on the outskirts of Boston, Massachusetts. She had been living alone with her father for so long that it seemed to be almost her entire lifetime. Her mother had passed away when Sandra was a girl of five and a half years, and the memory of her mother dissolved little by little every day. If it had not been for the faded photograph that Sandra kept on the table next to her bed, the visual memory of her mother may have been completely diminished.

When their cold mansion of a house was silent and still, in the moments just before drifting off to sleep, Sandra could hear her mother's sweet voice. It warmed Sandra's heart as she sang the old English folk song "Early one Morning." Sandra tried hard to keep her mother's memory alive by listening for her mother's song every night.

Sandra was nearly eighteen now and writing was one of the many interests she had developed over the years. It was because of this interest and the desire for companionship that she was compelled to start a diary. Her intelligence and maturity were far above that of the average eighteen-year-old. Also, due to the fact that her closet companion and best friend was her genius father, Sandra could, when she desired, be quite articulate. She had an extensive vocabulary for a girl of her age.

Sandra, dreamed of becoming a published author someday, despite the fact that women were solely expected to marry and have children. Careers were reserved for those unfortunate souls who weren't able to find a husband.

CHAPTER ONE
JANUARY

January 3, 1964

My father has just announced that he will be leaving me for as long as a year! He will be temporarily leaving his position as a Professor of Anthropology at Harvard University and going on a sabbatical to India. What bothered me the most was the way he told me. His tone was so nonchalant, his voice lacked any hesitation or any sign of regret. Much less any hint that he would miss me, his only child.

I do think it thoughtful that he gave me this diary though. This, he told me "is to aid in keeping you occupied in my absence."

January 7, 1964

My father left today. There was no drama, no tears. A brief exchange of kisses on the cheek and a farewell wave was the full extent of our goodbye. I was relieved that I was not going to be left completely alone. My aunt has come to care for me and our house. This was my first time meeting my Aunt Savita.

When she introduced herself, I would have thought an embrace would have been appropriate. To my dismay all that I received was a slight grin and a "Hello, I am very pleased to meet you."

I feel so lost and lonely in this monstrosity of a house. With just father and me living here and now just Aunt Savita and me. There is no question in my mind that this house is far too large for just two people.

Our closest neighbor lives a quarter of a mile away. I would have loved to live in a neighborhood where the houses were smaller, closer together, and there were other children to play with. Over the years I have brought this to my father's attention many times, to no avail. The reply I received was "Your mother loved this house, so we will keep it and that's that." I cannot bring myself to argue with that.

At least, now that I am nearly eighteen, having friends in the neighborhood is becoming less important. Many of my friends are getting their driver's licenses! Thank goodness, the distance between us is seemingly shrinking.

January 10, 1964

I have made every attempt to converse with my aunt. She is very quiet and withdrawn. To be frank, she seems to have a noticeable personality deficit. She doesn't interfere with my business, which I do appreciate, and I guess she doesn't expect me to interfere with hers. Fair enough. Although, it would be nice to have someone that I could confide in, or at least have a conversation with. She seems to be covered in a shroud of elusiveness.

January 16, 1964

I just realized that it has been six days since I last wrote. I've been so busy since school started again. Christmas break was the best ever. Despite the cold weather and all the snow, I went out with friends nearly every night. But it is time to slow down. It will be easy to stay in tonight; the snow is piling up just like my homework! A night by the fire doing homework will be nice for a change.

Although I'm not so sure about spending time in the house with Aunt Savita. She has been driving me bananas.

Every time the doorbell or telephone rings she will announce who it is before either of us answers it.

Anyway, I have tomorrow to look forward to; it is Friday night and my new friend Johnny is picking me up. He's taking me to the roller rink. Later, Gator!

January 18, 1964

Friday night at the roller rink was a gas! When Johnny and I danced to "Tutti Fruity" everyone at the rink stood to the side and watched us. It was absolutely out of this world!! Johnny is such a great dancer. He's such a hunk and so smart and talented. I feel amazed that he has any interest in little old me!

As we were dancing our eyes met and a feeling of sheer delight came over me. It was as if a chemist had mixed a formula. Johnny + Sandra = flying sparks! The perfect love potion. One that creates the ultimate happiness. I felt as if I were dancing on clouds as I made my way up the stairs, past my cranky aunt and to you, dear diary.

Speaking of Aunt Savita, she is definitely peculiar and some might even call her weird. Even after living here for 11 days, she still rarely speaks to me. I feel that she is completely unapproachable. Aside from announcing meal times, she doesn't speak to me unless it is an absolute necessity. She is a different looking woman. She has straight black, oily hair that is pulled back. It reminds me of the greaser's hair I saw when I was a little kid. Her face is narrow and she has a red dot between her eye brows. She must be all of 5'3 when she's not crouched over. She looks as though she weighs about 110 pounds soaking wet. Her big brown eyes have a deep sadness, and they are hallowed and sunken. It's as if she has had so much sorrow in her life that it has worn her down and she has no enthusiasm left in her. She wears the same gold, bell shaped earrings every day. Her complexion is dark, much darker than mine or my father's. I can't help but wonder why her features bear no resemblance to ours.

Well on an unrelated note, I heard today on the radio that designs for the tallest buildings in the world have been released. It will be an urban renewal project in lower Manhattan--New York City--and they will be called The World Trade Center Buildings. How exciting is that?

January 22, 1964

In our Social Studies class, we are having an interesting unit on extra sensory perception (ESP), witchcraft and superstitions. Today our lesson was about the Salem witch hunt. I find it so difficult to believe that nineteen people were hung because Protestant Christians thought that these poor souls were witches. This was over two hundred and fifty years ago but it happened so close to our home! Is that creepy or what? On Tuesday our class will be taking a field trip to Salem! I am about to jump right out of my skin I am so excited!

January 26, 1964

Yesterday was our trip to Salem. Boy, was it wild! Johnny is my closest friend in Social Studies class. So, naturally he was the one I hung out with. Our whole class along with our teacher, Mr. Rabin, took a ferry to Salem. When we arrived, we were told to pair up with a buddy and meet back at the ferry dock no later than 6:00pm, as that was when our chartered ferry departed.

Johnny is really a dream boat. Looking at him is like looking at a cool glass of water when you're dying of thirst. Plus, he's friendly, confident and outgoing. He has light, sandy brown hair, soulful brown eyes and a smile that makes my heart race like a ticking time bomb. He has a physique that matches his strong voice. Today I wrote Sandra + Johnny in hearts all over the inside cover of my notebook. I would just die of embarrassment if Johnny ever saw it.

When Mr. Rabin told us to pair off, Johnny grabbed my hand and joyfully pulled me away, exclaiming, "Let's go!" I admit I liked that, although I'm not sure that he realizes his own strength. I'm glad that my arm is still in its socket!

As we wandered aimlessly through the streets of Salem, the air became cooler. Before we knew it, we were surrounded by heavy mist. It was as if somehow this eerie haze was alive and welcoming us into its bizarre world. The musty scent, the obscure vision; I was totally engulfed in this peculiar ambiance. Everything seemed to be moving in slow motion as we made our way through the indistinct streets, and I felt as if I was a cast member in a horror show.

We trudged our way through the mist. We passed The House of the Seven Gables. This is the mysterious haunted house that Nathaniel Hawthorne wrote about in the book of the same name. It is said to still have tormented spirits wandering the halls. My entire body shuddered from the inside out.

I felt Johnny's hand on my shoulder and the heat that radiated from his palms. This gesture filled me with a sense of comfort that immediately calmed me.

Soon we came across the Wesley United Methodist Church. It was built in the early 1800's. Even the church had a creepy feel. The top of its steeple vanished in the fog. If it could speak, I imagine it would be screaming up to God, "Save me from this frightful place!"

We climbed up to Gallows Hill and saw the supposed spot where the accused witches were hanged. I had read that one by one they were hanged on the same tree. While we stood there, I thought of the torment that was endured at this very spot. Then, as if it were the voice of God expressing his disapproval about what had happened, there was an earth-shattering CLASH of thunder. It was so loud that my body shook from the vibration and frightened me back into a feeling of panic. I felt as if there was something evil right on our tail, ready to swoop down and scoop us up!

I think that even Johnny was startled. He squeezed my shoulder tightly as the ground trembled beneath our feet! I looked at him and realized that he was trying to hide his fear. Then, within seconds we were flooded by a horrific, intense downpour! The rain came hard, fast and cold. It felt like tiny needles relentlessly piercing my skin.

We raced through the streets of downtown Salem. I looked back as we ran and saw a bolt of lightning strike a tree a few feet from where we had stood just minutes before. I stopped abruptly, stunned, urging Johnny to a halt. Before our eyes, sparks swirled around the tree and small flames rose up as it split down the middle. We watched, paralyzed in astonishment, as half the tree along with its branches fell with a violent force to the ground.

Johnny pulled me along and we gained speed. We were now totally drenched and chilled to the bone. At last, we spotted an "OPEN" sign in the window of a small café, a sanctuary in our time of desperation. A wooden sign hung from a metal post outside the entrance that read "Ye Old Curiosity Shop and Eatery."

The café had European feel. It reminded me of a café where my father and I once had lunch, in Paris, near the Chandelles. Although the color scheme seemed a bit unusual; the tables were all black and the cushions were bright green. A very slight woman who looked to be older than anyone I had ever seen before greeted and seated us. She was very cordial, but she had an odd aura about her. She had a forced friendliness that didn't reveal what was behind her eyes. Her hair was ghostly white and her skin was shriveled. Her nose was long and crooked as if it had been broken many times in her long life. Her canine teeth were the only teeth visible as she gave us a wide grin, reminding me of the Jack O' Lantern my father carved last Halloween!

There were some very odd options on the menu, with names that had a supernatural theme. I guess it was all part of the tourist attraction.

The old woman came to take our order: a cauldron of clam chowder, sizzling snake sausage and a mystical malt. Johnny ordered the same with a side of deviled eggs. I also had a spot of licorice tea to "warm the cockles of my heart." This was a comforting expression I remember my mother often used. It was all wonderfully delicious!

When we were content with our nourishment and we had

warmed up, our host invited us into the back room to have a look around. We made our way through a makeshift door made of long chains of black beads. As we entered there was a strong unfamiliar scent and I asked our host what the aroma was. The old woman told us that it was her sable incense and that it was for sale at a very reasonable price, along with a wide variety of other scents.

As she showed us around, she explained to us that she was of the Wiccan religion—in other words a witch. She told us that in the Wiccan religion, rather than worshiping a god, they worship earth, nature and all that it gives us.

The room was illuminated with the glow of many candles. There were rows of shelves filled with knickknacks, candles, incense, jewelry, and what appeared to be antiques and various other curiosities. The items were labeled with price tags.

Across from these shelves there was a glass cabinet so tall that it nearly reached the ceiling. The sign in the center of the cabinet read:

APOTHOCARY: ELIXIRS, POTIONS, MEDICINES, OILS, HERBS

and other natural remedies.

Next to the cabinet there was a wall that looked weathered, and musty. The black paint was peeling and revealed the white wall behind it. It was as if someone had taken a giant potato peeler to it.

A massive spider web spread over a group of pictures. The center picture was a particularly large, framed painting of a young lady wearing a cameo brooch that looked much like the one my mother had on in the photograph I kept by my bed! I couldn't stop looking at her. The lady looked as if she could have been a younger version of my mother! The price of the painting was $18.00. It would leave me broke, but I couldn't resist. This painting needed to be mine.

The old woman wrapped up the painting in old newspapers, and then placed it in a green plastic bag.

Her eyes locked onto mine." To protect it from the elements," she said.

When I told her that the painting resembled my deceased mother, she told me that she had purchased the painting from a young woman many years ago.

She told me that the young woman resembled the lady in the painting. But she said that it was a long ago and that like paintings, memories can also fade. She gave me the bag as she explained "this is to protect it from the elements." I think that I'll always remember the ugly web of blue veins that rose up through her white, crepe- paper- thin skin.

As we left, the rain was letting up, but the downpour was replaced by a brisk howling wind, ominous and terrifying, like it could have been beckoning a group of spirits to gather for some kind of ungodly ritual. The sky quickly filled with the darkness of a moonless night, and even with Johnny as my protector, a fearful feeling came over me. I felt as if the wind could pick us up at any moment and hurl us around until we landed in a sinister version of the city of OZ.

We had lost track of the time. It was 5:40. We had only twenty minutes to catch the last ferry out of Salem!

Johnny told me not to worry. He assured me that he would get us to the ferry in time. I wasn't completely convinced that he knew the way back to the ferry. But if I had to be lost in Salem with anyone, I'd chose Johnny.

After a short walk we came across a modern brick building with SALEM HIGH SCHOOL in bold letters on the side. A figure dressed all in black was slowly approaching us and I began to feel nauseated as he drew closer. Johnny didn't seem worried in the least.

As the figure came into clear view, I could see it was a really good-looking guy I'd say that he was a high school sophomore or junior. As he approached, he waved to us. He greeted us with a friendly smile and introduced himself as Damian. He asked us where we were from and told us that he went to Salem High and he had just come from the Witches practice! This, he explained, was the name of his school's basketball team.

Time was really becoming short now. We asked Damian for directions to the ferry, and he told us it was just down the hill. This was the first I time I had seen Johnny really agitated. He shouted, "Let's cut out of this gloomy place!" He grabbed my hand again and nearly pulling me over, he dashed us down the hill! When we reached the bottom of the hill, we saw the ferry begin to pull away from the dock.

"Wait, wait for us!" Johnny's voice was strong and authoritative. It sounded to me like the shouts of an Army Boot Camp Drill Sargent.

My heart felt as if it was going to leap right out of my chest! We were both relieved when the ferry immediately began to turn back for us, and we boarded safely.

Well, after telling that long story, dear diary, I am ready to visit Mr. Sandman.

CHAPTER TWO
FEBRUARY

February 3, 1964

I'm sorry that I haven't written, dear diary. I have been busy again. I compared the painting I bought in Salem with the photo I have of my mother at my bedside. It is, beyond a shadow of a doubt, a painting of my mother! But why was it in a shop in Salem? I am determined to find out!

I have been preparing for a research report in my Social Studies Class. I have decided to do my report on Psychic Powers and Extra Sensory Perception or in brief, ESP. I have checked out eight books on the subject from the library. Although I'd love nothing more than to continue writing, I must get some reading done. Later, dear diary.

February 6, 1964

My aunt has all the signs of having ESP. I have really immersed myself in the subject. I am becoming quite knowledgeable (if I do say so myself). Lately, sleeping alone in this house with Aunt Savita has been, well, shall I say, unsettling. I hear my mother's voice in the middle of the night, not only singing but also calling out my name. I have gone looking for her and I have seen transparent figures of her. She has her hands outstretched as if she is longing for a hug. She always appears in the living room in a ghost like form, just like the ghosts that I've seen portrayed in the movies. After a few moments she vanishes into thin air. When I see her, I feel both a sense of warmth and fear. I want so much to believe that it is my mother, but the sensible side of me keeps telling me, Sandra, you know ghosts aren't real!

Tonight, I'll be attending a club meeting of "The Mystics". Johnny and some other students from my Social Studies class formed. The idea for the name came from our recent visit to Salem. See ya later alligator!

February 8, 1964

As I have delved even deeper into the study of the sixth sense, aka extra sensory perception, it has become more and more evident that my aunt does, in fact, have psychic powers. The Mystics are holding a special meeting next week. We will be conducting a séance. Because of the extensive research I have done, I was elected to act as the medium. We will attempt to make contact with my mother. The thought of contacting her excites me so much that mere mortal words cannot describe the feelings that are overtaking me!

February 10, 1964

It was just another chaotic Monday today. Although last night was amazing. I went over to Johnny's house. He had Mike and Cheri, Bill and Rachel, and Todd and Alice over to watch the Ed Sullivan show on his new 21-inch color TV. They are all members of The Mystics. A new pop group called the Beatles were the show's special guests. All the young people are going completely out of their minds for this British band!

Johnny's dad came in the room and mumbled, "Long haired beatniks!"

The Beatles are really groovy musicians who came all the way from Liver Pool, England. I think that Paul is the cutest. I love his smile and the sparkle in his eyes. I'm also crazy about their accent. It reminds me a bit of my mother. My favorite number was the first one, "I Wanna Hold Your Hand." Johnny took my hand and held it tightly through their entire performance. Apparently, the song is on the Top 40. I've heard that because of the mass popularity of this group and other British bands who are coming to America, the papers are calling it "The British Invasion!" Isn't that silly?

February 12, 1964

Last night we had the séance here at the house. Although I am far from a professional medium, I believe I did quite a good job. All eight of the core members of The Mystics were there. We were all gathered around our dining table. My aunt stayed hidden away in her bedroom. We had the lights off and the room was illuminated solely by the flicker of two candles on either end of the table. There must have been a slight breeze coming from the window for the flames moved around as if they, too, were in search of my mother's spirit.

I was seated at the head of the table and Johnny was by my side. In the center of the table I had placed my mother's photo, her painting and her wedding dress which I had folded and placed in between the photo and the painting. I set the cup my mother always used to drink her morning "cuppa" (cup of tea) next to the dress.

I began with a prayer:

"God if there are any evil spirits in our midst, protect us from them. Please allow me to have contact with my mother."

As we held hands with one another I called to my mother, pleading to her that she make contact with me. The rest of the group called for her by name.

"Cassandra are you here? If you are here please, make yourself known!"

There was no sign of her presence. I asked her to turn the cup to the right if she was here. But still, there was nothing. Then, as a last attempt to reach her I began singing the song I had heard her sing so many times in the past.

"Early one morning just as the sun was rising, I heard a young maid singing in the valley below. Oh, don't deceive me, oh never leave me, how could you use a poor maiden so."

Just as I began completing the final verse, a whirl of wind burst the window open! The shutters clanged violently, back and forth, back and forth, banging relentlessly against the house! A cold chill chattered its way down my spine, followed by a familiar feeling of warmth and security, the kind of feeling a small child might feel when she falls down and her mother picks her up to provide comfort. It was a feeling that I hoped would never end.

Suddenly, the entire group let out a collective gasp. I saw a look of utter shock on each face. Alice had one hand over her mouth as she pointed to the cup which was now on the floor, upright and undamaged! It had turned to the right!

Then the candles went out.

We sat there silently for a moment in the pitch darkness. Johnny then jumped up quickly.

"I'll get the lights!" he exclaimed.

I think it's safe to say that we all felt a welcome relief that our adventure had come to an end for the evening. Everyone departed immediately after that, even Johnny. I think that everyone was still a little shocked. I wasn't quite as shocked as my fellow club members. For in my heart of hearts, I guess I had known that we would make contact with mum.

February 13, 1964

I am so thrilled; Johnny passed his driver's license test today! Tomorrow is Valentine's Day and the world is our oyster!

February 15, 1964

Last night I went out with Johnny. He came to the door holding a bouquet of a dozen red and yellow roses! As I looked at him standing inside the door with such a regal demeanor, my heart filled with love, my mind raced with excitement and my lungs endured a feeling of breathlessness! I couldn't believe that this handsome man was here for me! I was wearing a red silk gown I had found in mum's closet, and although it was more fitted than the dresses that I am used to wearing, it suited me perfectly. I had my long brown hair pulled up in tight bun. I was also wearing makeup which is a rarity for me. I felt like a princess walking down the grand stair case as her prince awaits. Although I had never felt so beautiful, I was a bit uncomfortable. I felt as if I didn't deserve to be so beautiful.

Johnny's eyes met mine and the chemistry was so overwhelming that after a few moments I had to look away.

Johnny then blurted out, "You look swell!" That comment made me loosen up and smile.

Aunt Savita then came down and took a snap shot of

us to send to my father. I could tell by her enthusiasm that she was excited to try out her new Kodak Instamatic camera. I had given it to her for her birthday just a few days ago. Although she didn't have many gifts, this seemed to be her favorite.

Johnny took me to one of the oldest and most historic restaurants in all of Boston. During dinner he made a romantic champagne toast to our future together. When we had finished our dinner, the waiter approached with a covered plate on a silver tray.

Johnny's voice was filled with anticipation. "That must be our dessert already!"

Then, the waiter set the plate in front of me. He reached down with his white glove and removed the cover. I was fully expecting a delicious cake. But instead, to my delight, there before me I saw Johnny's class ring! At that very moment, Johnny asked me if I would be his steady girl. Needless to say, I accepted. But, with the condition that we could still have a cake for dessert!

We talked for hours. We discussed school, sports, the future, and finally my aunt, the séance and the painting. He is going to bring my aunt's ESP up to the other members of the Mystics. He said that he would talk to them about researching it further. Also, I told him of how I still yearned for that warm, secure feeling that came over me at the séance.

As we left the restaurant and walked to Johnny's car, he took my hand and pulled me gently toward him. We gave each other a wonderfully warm embrace. He followed this by giving me a little kiss on my cheek. He told me that if that wasn't enough of a warm secure feeling for me, then he could arrange another séance. I then became a blushing teenage girl and let out a little giggle. I think that I am quite possibly the happiest girl in all of Massachusetts. My guy certainly has an 18K heart!

February 16, 1964

Today would have been my mother's 40th birthday. I asked Johnny if he would mind bringing me to the cemetery so I could leave some lilies of the valley on her grave. They were her favorite flowers. Father and I try to keep up the garden she planted. It still flourishes with the perennials from all those years ago. As long as I can remember there have been two black wrought iron chairs next to each other in the garden. Every Sunday morning, no matter what the weather, I would see my father sitting out there. He would sit in the chair on the north side, often with his face in his hands. How he must miss her today on her birthday. I do wish that I could be with him.

Johnny told me that he would be happy to take me to my mother's grave site. We drove in an awkward silence to the cemetery.

It was a beautiful day for the middle of February. The sun was shining bright and there was a mild breeze. The taste of spring was in the air. It was just enough to wet my pallet and leave me longing for more.

I knelt down at my mother's grave; I placed the lilies down in front of her name. At that very moment a beautifully vibrant, red cardinal flew into view. The clouds above me spread apart as if they were theatre curtains at the opening act of a play. As the clouds parted, a bright stream of light shone down directly in front of the tombstone. It was as if my mother's warmth was reaching down to make her presence and love known to me. The cardinal perched directly in front of me, on the center of my mother's tombstone. It then chirped a little tune: shoo... followed by multiple, quick, little tweets: tweet, tweet, tweet, tweet, tweet, tweet, tweet, tweet and again, shoo…tweet, tweet, tweet…

I felt a closeness to this bird so, despite my knowledge of the dangers of handling wild birds, I gently pushed my finger under its belly. Without any hesitation it hoped right on! For just a moment it stared at me. It looked me directly in the eyes. Then with a flutter it hopped onto my shoulder. It nudged its tiny head against my neck and I felt the tickle of its soft feathers against the underside of my chin. It then flew away. I felt that same secure feeling of a mother's warmth as I gazed with wonder into the sky, following the bird's flight as it went higher and higher until it was a tiny speck.

As I stared at the sky, still mesmerized by the little bird, the gap between the clouds closed up. The stream of light disappeared as quickly as it had come. Johnny and I walked away, arm and arm. We were both awestruck and speechless at what had just occurred. I felt a bit light-headed. I told Johnny that I needed some time alone. I didn't want to be rude, but my head was swirling around. I felt as if I were the pilot of a dive bomber that had come within inches of a crash landing.

When we arrived home, Johnny walked me to the door. We each said a simple goodbye and he gently squeezed my hand.

The sitting room was warmed slightly by a small fire trying desperately to stay alive. I poked the fire several times and restored it to life. I then collapsed fireside in my father's favorite over-stuffed armchair. I felt comforted by the old familiar aroma of his pipe tobacco. This scent lingered in the old chair and I could envision my father sitting there, reading the paper and enjoying his pipe.

Out of nowhere, an overwhelming feeling of sorrow engulfed me. I felt like a boat with a gigantic leak with all the energy and ambition draining out of my body.

My father has always taught me to be stoic and courageous in the face of adversity and to "keep a stiff upper lip." So, being the good obedient daughter that I am, I seldom let go and cry. Tonight, was different. I let my emotions take over. I began to sob and sob, and when I should have been done, I sobbed some more. Eventually, with my throat and head swollen, my tears ran dry.

Then a very unexpected event occurred. I heard the stairs speak with their old familiar creek. Aunt Savita, carrying a candle, was making her way gingerly down our grand stair case. She was so slow and careful that one would think the stairs were made of glass. She entered the room and to my astonishment she sat down next to me. She placed her arm around my shoulder with tenderness. There was a beating heart in my aunt after all! I felt her stale breath on my face as she invaded my personal space. She told me that she knows how much I miss my mother and said that she also misses her. She asked me if I had ever been told the story of how my parents had first met. She definitely had my attention!

She proceeded to tell me the story in a soft patient voice.

"Your parents," she said, met on the Queen Mary just after WWII. There was a new law passed that would allow 100 Asian Indians naturalization in the United States. Nigel—your dad—and I left India in hopes of starting a new and better life in the US. We made our way to London where we were told that the Cunard Line was hiring workers for the Queen Mary. In exchange for their labor they would be allowed free passage to the US. They were in the process of bringing European war brides, Jewish holocaust survivors and other more affluent travelers to the United States of America. We took a train to Southampton where we applied to the Cunard Line and were delighted to be hired!

"Your father began his career at sea as a dishwasher. On the third day, one of the waiters became too seasick to deliver the food to your mother's table. Nigel stepped in. His English was perfect; his manners were as impeccable as a British Lord's. His work ethic was irreproachable. Within a few days your father was promoted to lead waiter.

"With his promotion we were not only given free passage but he was also earning quite a lot of extra money. We were able set it aside for our new start in America. I was not as fortunate as your father. I remained a maid throughout the voyage and I spent my days cleaning the rooms of the first-class passengers.

"Your father waited on your mother and her parents' table for every meal. He and your mother developed quite the romantic flirtation. He even won over your mother's parents, your Grandmother Sarah and Grandfather William. Nigel and Cassandra would dance the evenings away blissfully, while I remained a lonely wall flower. Your father let everyone believe that he was an Englishman and no one questioned him. This was not only because of his mannerisms but he also had pale skin and Northern European features.

"You, my dear Sandra," my aunt said, "were born on your parents' first wedding anniversary!"

To my dismay, Aunt Savita then paused. She told me in a hushed voice so soft and sweet it could lull an infant to sleep that it was time for me to get to bed.

February 17, 1964

I awoke this morning with a new zest and enthusiasm for life. I felt as if my aunt had begun to come out of her shell and that perhaps now, we could become friends. Instead of her usual, "Breakfast is served," she called out, "Sandra, come and have your breakfast!" Everything was better, the sun shone a little brighter, the birds chirped with a little more enthusiasm, the taste of breakfast was more satisfying, and the world seemed to be an altogether happier place!

Johnny was waiting outside to take me to school. I walked out of my house just as he was approaching the gate.

He announced, "Your chariot awaits you, Madame!" I was thrilled to see a shiny new fire engine red Ford Galaxy! He said that his parents had given it to him as a pre-high school graduation gift! Riding to school in his brand-new car, coddled in the leather bucket seats, with the windows down and radio cranked up made me feel like a teenage American princess! When we pulled into the school parking lot kids seemed to crawl out of the woodwork. Everyone wanted to have a look at the brand-new Galaxy! Johnny beamed with pride as he showed off his new car and his new girl. I don't know how this day could have been any better!

February 20, 1964

My life has changed so much for the better in the past few days dear diary. I have been having actual daily conversations with my aunt! She even bought us a 19" color television set! Prior to this we only had my father's 16" black and white TV which he kept in his study.

Last night we watched an hour-long news program. The Civil Rights Bill passed the House today so the show was mainly about the Civil Rights movement. They did also discuss the Viet Nam War. There was talk of America entering the war and I imagine it was a topic of conversation in the majority of American households.

Aunt Savita predicts that the war will go on for another 11 years and that the North Vietnamese will be the final victors. It is frightening to think about. I am very thankful that Johnny seems to have no interest in joining the military. Although, if Aunt Savita is right and this war goes on, there is always the possibility that he might be drafted eventually. I don't even want to think about that.

February 21, 1964

I am filled with the warm glow of anticipation. This Saturday is my eighteenth birthday! I am not expecting anything from Aunt Savita, but I'm sure that at the very least Johnny is taking me out to dinner. My greatest hope is that I will hear from my father on my birthday and what would have been his and my mum's wedding anniversary!

February 24, 1964

Today was my 18th birthday. It was a day full of wonderful surprises. I think that it is safe to say that this was the very best day of my entire life! Johnny made me a picnic lunch. Since it was too cold outside, he took me to the enclosed atrium he has in his backyard. It was perfect. It looked and felt as if we were outside without the chill.

As the sun streamed in, we feasted on all the food which he had prepared himself. We had assorted fruits, sandwiches, chips and cookies. When we had our fill of his tasty picnic, Johnny said he that we should have a special marker to remember this day. He led me outside to a big oak tree in the middle of the yard. He took out his pocket knife and carefully carved a large heart. On the inside of the heart he wrote "Johnny + Sandra FOREVER". I thanked him and gave him a little peck on the cheek.

To my dismay and shock, he responded by telling me that he was busy this evening and that he would have to take me home! I was crushed! I didn't want to be selfish, controlling or smothering but it was my birthday and I had assumed that we would do something together this evening. As we drew closer and closer to home, my loneliness and sorrow grew by leaps and bounds. I could feel my heart sink like a treasure chest falling slowly to the ocean floor.

By the time we reached my house I could feel the moisture building up in my eyes. A tear trickled down my cheek. I thought to myself that I had begun this day with such humble expectations and yet I was going to end it disappointed! As we reached home and I began to open the car door, Johnny gave me the most kind and compassionate look that one could ever imagine. He then went around the car to open my door. He walked me through the gate to my front door and gave me an ever so soft and sweet little kiss on my lips. It was my first real kiss! The feeling the kiss gave me, dear diary was so marvelous, such a feeling of jubilation came over me! I was in a state of pure bliss! I felt as if I had been knocking on Heaven's door and I was finally let in! What a marvelous 18th birthday gift!

My heart was singing! My mind was soaring! As I happily swooned, with my head in the clouds, Johnny put his arm around me and opened my front door for me. To my astonishment, I heard what sounded to me like a choir of angels singing, "Happy birthday to you, Happy Birthday to you!" My aunt was the first person I noticed. She stood there, looking taller than usual, with a smile that said, "I am very satisfied with my accomplishment." I ran to her and hugged her tightly. There must have been twenty or thirty of my friends, classmates, and neighbors behind her. I was so thrilled! My stomach felt as if it were filled with little butterflies trying to break free.

I then saw a rather short, stalky, dark skinned, man coming out from the kitchen. He was dressed up in a tuxedo and wearing a grey turban. A silly memory entered my mind. When my mother saw my father, all dressed up one day, she said, "My, aren't you all dressed up like a tuppeny ham bone!" I asked my father years later what on earth this meant. He said that mum had told him that it was an old English saying having to do with the garnish and dressing around the ham-bone when serving ham at a party. Thinking of this conjured up a silly picture in my mind and made me laugh out loud, in-appropriately!

The debonair hambone man was carrying a three-tier cake with the candles lit. He was headed directly toward me. I heard several shouts requesting me to "make a wish". It was a very easy decision for me to choose a wish. The only thing that could possibly make this day any better was to hear from my father. I made my wish. I took one deep breath and I blew out all eighteen candles with one strong blow! Johnny then told everyone to give it up for his favorite girl. Gee whiz, did they ever give it up! They gave and gave for what seemed to be an eternity. Of course, in reality, it was probably less than a minute!

The hambone man then came out with a cart filled with gifts that were all wrapped in dazzling paper, with beautiful colors, shiny bows and fancy ribbons.

The very moment the gifts were placed next to me, in front of everyone, Johnny got down on one knee. He had a smile on his face that was so warm it felt as if it was wrapping around me like a warm blanket. I had a feeling as to what was going to happen next, but at the same time I could hardly believe it!

"Sandra," he said, "When I imagine my future it is always with you by my side. There is no greater honor that I could possibly achieve then you accepting my hand in marriage. Sandra, my love, will you accompany me in the journey of life and become my wife?"

Johnny then pulled from his pocket the most beautiful diamond engagement ring that I had ever seen! I was stunned! I became all choked up. There were several girls in my class that were engaged already, but I never thought that I would be one of them! I feel that I am too young, there is so much that I want to do with my life! There are so many dreams that I have yet to fulfill.

But I think the world of Johnny and I can't imagine my life without him in it. I tried to utter a yes, but a very weak, pathetic, little sound came out. I am certain that it was inaudible to the crowd. A tear of joy rolled down my check as he placed the ring on my finger, kissed my hand, and held me in a tender embrace.

The hambone man then put the song "Earth Angel" on our stereo. Johnny and I danced and others followed. Even my aunt danced with the hambone man! After several enchanting hours of dancing and romance, the guests began to depart. I felt as if I were Cinderella, and at the stroke of midnight my life would return to normal and reality would rear its head.

Our old grandfather clock did strike midnight. Johnny, Aunt Savita and I were the only people left. I thanked them with great zeal for making this the best day of my life. Johnny gave me a kiss on the hand, and another warm tender kiss on the lips. He followed this with an embrace and he bid a fond farewell to his bride-to-be.

February 25, 1964

We never did get around to opening the gifts last night. My aunt and I reserved that pleasure for today. I received many thoughtful and special gifts. With the exception of Johnny's ring, there were none quite as special to me as Aunt Savita's and my father's. Aunt Savita gave me a cameo brooch, but it wasn't just any cameo brooch; it was the one mother was wearing in the painting! Aunt Savita said that my mother treasured it and had asked her to give it to me on my eighteenth birthday. This cameo, I was told, originally belonged to my great grandmother and it was carved in her likeness. I will treasure it forever!

I thought that this would be an opportune time to tell my aunt about the painting and ask her if she had any idea why it would have been for sale in Salem. A look of amazement came over her face and she asked to see the painting. I fetched the painting and as I handed it to her, she grasped it with a slight tremor in her hand. She smoothed her finger gently over the painting. Then she began to tell me another story of the past.

She told me that she could recall the day in which the picture was painted. She said that it was painted aboard the Queen Mary.

"Your father was a very happy man at this time in his life. He was being paid well, working his position of lead waiter. He had been courting your mother. Outside the dining room one evening the ship had a French painter. For a fee he would paint passenger's portraits. Your father had paid the painter in advance. He gave the painter instructions. The painter should tell your mother that he would be most honored if she would allow him to paint her portrait. Your father never let on to your mother that he had paid the painter nearly three days' wages! As far as I know your mother believed that the painting was done complements of the painter. She did cherish the painting, but your parents must have sold it. I know that they were very short of money while your father was earning his master's degree. I never thought that I would see this painting again! Nigel will be ever so pleased when he learns that you now have it!"

Then there was my father's gift. It was perfect! It was a new electronic device called a portable tape recorder. Inside there was a cassette tape. My father had written on it: "Happy 18th Birthday to my Sandra! With Love Dad".

As I listened to the tape the sound of his voice soothed my loneliness for him. He had many questions for me. To my surprise Johnny had asked his permission for my hand in marriage. My father told me that he had complete faith in my ability to make the correct decision.

"Whatever decision you make," he said. "I will support you."

He showered me with complements regarding what a strong, sensible, intelligent young woman I had grown into and how much I was like my mother.

He also mentioned how proud he was of me. The only thing that slightly troubled me was his goodbye. He told me that although he didn't expect it, if anything should happen delaying or preventing his return, I should depend on my aunt for love, support and guidance. I'm not certain what he meant by this. Having already lost my mother, I can't even think of the possibility of losing my father too!

CHAPTER THREE
MARCH

March 10, 1964

I apologize for waiting so long to update you dear diary.

Things have been going well at school and at home. Johnny was accepted into Harvard and I was accepted into Boston University. Harvard was Johnny's first choice and Boston University was the only college that I applied to. Aunt Savita has been seeing the hambone man who I will now refer to by his given name, Raj. He has been coming over after work most days. They play cards or watch television. I haven't yet mustered up the courage to ask her about their friendship. It is on my to-do list.

Johnny and I have discussed setting a date for our wedding. He has agreed to wait until I finish college, although he would prefer it if we were married yesterday!

March 12, 1964

I had a nice in-depth conversation with Aunt Savita today. I asked her about her friendship with the Raj. She told me that he was a friend from her childhood in India and that he has just recently moved to the U.S. She said that they have been reminiscing and rekindling their friendship. She said that she is helping him adjust to his new life here. Like her, she said, he has never married.

I also asked her if she had any idea why my father had put the notion in my head that his return could be delayed or thwarted. My aunt, I thought, was somewhat evasive in her answer. She replied that she had complete faith that he would return home by January of next year as expected.

I also asked her if she had the gift of ESP. She said that

she did have a gift, and she could at times predict the future. She said that from the time she was a small child her parents had nurtured and assisted her in developing this psychic power. She said that God had blessed all the women in their family with this gift for generations. She told me that she was sworn to keep this gift as a family secret. If word were to get out regarding her powers, she could be accused of being a witch. She was told that one never knows when such witch hunts could happen again. History, she explained, has a way of repeating itself.

I can't help but wonder, since the women of our family have passed this gift down from generation to generation, then what happened with me? Am I not a woman of this family? Also, why is my skin nearly as pale as a ghost? I know that I may have inherited my skin color from my mother, and although not quite as pale as I am, my father also has a fair complication.

I think that I will say good night dear diary. I may lay awake for a time and try to sort some of this out.

March 15, 1964

Today in Social Studies we talked about Jack Ruby being found guilty of murdering Lee Harvey Oswald, the top suspect for the assassination of John F Kennedy. It was the first ever televised trial.

Also, our unit on Witchcraft, ESP and Superstitions has come to an end. I hope to receive an A. I certainly put a lot of effort into the class. Although, I didn't mind in the least and I enjoyed it more than any other class that I have ever taken. Our new unit is on Family History. Our first assignment is to write a report on our own family history. This should prove to be quite interesting!

I feel I know very little about our family's history except for what Aunt Savita has told me. I am especially lacking in the knowledge of my mother's and my father's family prior to immigrating to the USA. I am so psyched that if it wasn't nearly 9:00 pm I'd start tonight!

March 17, 1964

I walked home from school today. Johnny had a debate team event. After the long walk, I was exhausted. I must have had at least ten pounds of books with me. When I finally made it home, I saw a Junker, parked in our driveway. It was an old grey pickup truck.

As I entered the house, my aunt was coming up the stairs from our bomb shelter. There was a man so close behind her that if he had a slight stumble, she might have flown forward and been injured. The man had an exotic look about him. He appeared to be Asian Indian. He was grey bearded and steely eyed. He wore a bright, orange turban.

As the man raced up the stairs, he glared at me. His stare felt as if he was piercing me with tiny daggers. The look sent chills up and down my spine. My aunt looked disheveled as she hurried up the stairs. You could see beads of sweat forming on her forehead. Her right cheek was red, as if she had been slapped. If it were not for the deliberate smile she managed to scrounge up for me, I would have run out the door screaming for help. I wondered if I was making the right decision, because it was clear to me that the smile was deliberate and not natural.

The very next moment, the doorbell rang, and I ran to open it. It was Raj! He ran to my aunt, embraced her and asked her if she was alright. She told him that she was. He then turned to the man with the orange turban, grabbed him by the arm and led him with a rough determination out the door. I heard shouting back and forth in Hindi. I watched in horror from the window as the turbaned man took his fist and laid a forceful punch right into Raj's stomach! Raj doubled over slightly but he managed to keep his footing. Raj then transformed into Mighty Man! He punched the turbaned man with immense power! First in the face and then in the stomach! The turbaned man fell to the ground like a sack of potatoes. The heroic conqueror then strutted like a proud peacock toward the house. Aunt Savita ran out to Raj and they held each other tightly. The two walked back into the house, Raj, leaning slightly on Aunt Savita for support. As the three of us watched from the window, the turbaned man hobbled his way back to his truck and left.

March 18, 1964

It happened just minutes ago. I was peeking in on Raj and my Aunt Savita in the great room. As gently as a ballerina, I tiptoed back to my room so they wouldn't find out that I was watching. What I witnessed was incredibly sweet and romantic! The lights were dim. For several moments the only noise to be heard was the fire, crackling and snapping. Raj got down on one knee. He took my aunt's hand and said in a deep, soft voice, "Say yes my love, and grow old with me, for the two of us, the best days are yet to be." He then pulled a box from his pocket and placed a diamond ring on Aunt Savita's finger.

March 19, 1964

I mustered up the courage to ask my aunt about the turbaned man. I felt honored that she decided to confide in me.

"This," she told me, "is the story that has been passed down." She explained it to me in a methodical tone. "It took place nearly 70 years ago in my homeland. It was near Calcutta in West Bengal, India. Your grandfather, Aryan, was playing with a neighbor boy, Rudra. Our home was close to a river. Aryan and Rudra had gone to the river to play. They were using sticks as swords and pretending that they were dueling British soldiers. Their play became increasingly rough. Aryan had knocked Rudra's stick out of his hand. Aryan had won the duel and pointed his stick at Rudra's chest. Rudra lost his footing and fell into the river. Aryan did not realize that Rudra didn't know how to swim. As Rudra cried for help, Aryan jumped in to rescue him.

"Rudra, was being carried down currant toward the rapids. As Rudra flailed wildly, Aryan caught hold of him. They were but a stone's throw away from reaching the treacherous rapids. Aryan dragged Rudra to shore only to find that he was no longer breathing. Aryan carried Rudra on his back all the way to Rudra's family home. Needless to say, Rudra's parents were distraught, for there was no life left in Rudra.

"A few days later, Aryan's parents—your great grandparents—paid a visit to and spoke with Rudra's mother and father. Rudra's parents agreed not to tell the police. You see, because our part of India was under British rule, the Magistrate could have sentenced Aryan to a lifetime of hard labor. So that Rudra's family would keep this incident hidden from the police, your great grandparents agreed to pay a substantial monthly sum to Rudra's family.

"These payments continued all throughout your great grandfather's life. Aryan, your grandfather, was then forced to take over the payments. Rudra's family increased their demands every few years. They claimed that this was only fair because of inflation. Your father feared that when his father, Aryan, passed away, he would be expected to continue the payments.

"Nigel and I had hoped that moving to the USA would free us from this curse. The same year that your mother passed away, Aryan also passed away. We had thought that surely now our financial obligation to Rudra's family would cease. Unfortunately, Rudra's family had found out our address here, in America and we received a letter from their family requesting payment. Your father reluctantly continued payments for several years, until he finally decided enough is enough.

"The trip your father is currently on is a sabbatical and he will be lecturing at the university, but he is also determined to put an end to this financial burden while he is there."

She went on to say that the orange turbaned man worked for Rudra's family and they sent him here to extort a hefty lump sum from my father. He claimed that it was back pay.

"When I told him that we had nothing to give," she continued, "he became like a pot boiling over. He called me a name that I won't repeat. He then thrust the back of his hand across my face with so much force that I tumbled to the floor! Fear trembled through my bones. I then blurted out in desperation that I would contact your father and convince him to wire us the money."

She then told me it was long past both our bedtimes and we had best get to bed.

I have so many questions but I think that I should take some time to absorb all this new information. I'll sleep on it. Good night dear diary.

March 22, 1964

I have had a great few days. I have been so busy that I haven't had time to write. I have been concerned about my Aunt Savita and my father, but I also have had many distractions.

I have some really far out news! We are having an essay contest at school. The essay subject is "Why we would like to attend the World's Fair." The top ten essay writers will attend the 1964 New York World's Fair! The chaperone will be our Social Studies teacher again, Mr. Rabin. I am going to get started on my essay right away!

March 24, 1964

I have been working on my World's Fair Essay diligently; it is due next week. My Social Studies Family History report is due in 3 weeks. I am afraid, dear diary, that you will have to take a back seat!

March 26, 1964

Johnny and I went to Al's Drive-in last night. Word has spread regarding our engagement and it seems that half the school was there congratulating us. It was such a magical feeling. While everyone was congratulating us, "I Wonder Why" and "Teenager in Love" played through the drive-in speakers.

Our bliss then came to an abrupt end when one of the waitresses, Cindy, who is a friend of mine, was roller skating to Johnny's car, bringing us our food order. She tripped on something and fell. She landed just outside Johnny's car. Without a moment's hesitation, Johnny rushed to her aid. She seemed to be injured.

I was proud that Johnny was so helpful but at the same time I had a slight twinge of jealously. I suppose it was because he was giving another girl attention. The manager called an ambulance and I have heard that she is still in the hospital. I plan on visiting her tomorrow.

Johnny is also entering the World's Fair contest.

Wouldn't it be choice if we both won!

March 27, 1964

Johnny and I went to the hospital straight from school to visit Cindy today. The good news is that she is doing well. She broke her collar bone, but she should be back to school in a week or so.

The bad news is, in the next hospital room was Aunt Savita! She was visiting Raj! Apparently, he came to our house to visit Aunt Savita and out from behind our bushes came the turbaned man again. He had a tire iron and swung it repeatedly at Raj. Raj fought back and both men were injured. Raj assured me that he was just sore and had some cuts and bruises, and that with a few days of rest and relaxation and he would be just fine. Aunt Savita called the police as soon as she saw the turbaned man. He was promptly arrested and taken to jail.

March 28, 1964

Tomorrow is Easter Sunday. On Easter, my father and I would usually just have a nice ham dinner and a relaxing afternoon. Perhaps we would play a game of Scrabble, a game of chess, and in the evening, we would sit by the fire as he read me stories written by Charles Dickens, Mark Twain, Nathaniel Hawthorne, or Ernest Hemingway.

Well, this Easter would be much different. Johnny asked me to go to Easter Sunday church service at a church in downtown Boston with him and his family. He also invited me to have lunch at their house following the church service. I am very excited. I vaguely recall going to Easter and Christmas service with my mother before she passed away, but I haven't been to church since. Mainly, because father has never brought it up. I told Johnny that I would be delighted. I was concerned that Aunt Savita would be lonely, but she assured me that she would be fine. Raj, she said, was taking her out for Chinese.

March 29, 1964

Today was Easter Sunday and what a miraculous day it was! I went to church with Johnny, his mother, father and his 9-year-old sister. I felt like the cat's pajamas in my new spring dress. With my heels on I was nearly as tall as Johnny. My dress had a full skirt with large violet, blue and red flowers. It had a cropped matching jacket with ¾ length sleeves. I wore a tightly woven white straw hat. Artificial flowers of blue, violet, yellow, and red adorned the wide brim.

When Johnny picked me up, he looked so handsome in his gray suit! I felt as if we had just walked out of a fashion catalog! Johnny's family met us at the church. I was slightly nervous about meeting his parents but they were warm and friendly. His dad looked like an older version of Johnny. He was tall, with a handsome albeit care-worn face. His eyes were brown and soulful just like Johnny's and he carried himself with the same confidence. His hair was black with a distinguished bit of graying at the temples. He shook my hand gently. I can see where Johnny got his gentlemanly mannerisms.

His mother was an absolutely beautiful and elegant lady. She seemed as graceful as Lady Bird Johnson as she gave me a formal hug. His adorable little sister gave me a wide grin and handed me a daisy. Her name is Stacy and she told me in a sweet, quiet little voice that Johnny had told her that it would be alright if she asked me if she could be the flower girl at our wedding. I told her that I would be delighted to have her as the flower girl, but I also mentioned that it wouldn't be for another four years and by that time she might prefer to be my bride's maid instead. That statement seemed to impress the whole family and we cheerfully made our way into the sanctuary.

I can't remember ever being in such a beautiful building. The stained-glass windows were absolutely breathtaking! It had a high vaulted ceiling and there, perched above the window on a beam, was a red cardinal! As we walked down the aisle the organ played. The music was not familiar to me and I felt a bit out of place. Everyone seemed to know exactly what to say, how to respond to the minister in unison, and when to sit, kneel and stand. I struggled to follow along. The first song the choir and congregation sang was "Christ the

Lord Has Risen Today." It was so moving that I felt as if God himself was looking down on us with pleasure. The minister gave a very inspiring and moving sermon. So much so that I was nearly brought to tears.

Following the sermon, the minster prepared to give the congregation communion. Everything was still and silent with the exception of the cardinal singing its little heart out. Just as the minister poured the wine into the challis, the cardinal swooped down and landed on the side of the silver cup! It sang again, shoo...tweet, tweet, tweet, tweet, tweet. It took a sip of wine, bobbed its head back and forth and up and down, as if to shake off the excess wine. Deliberately, it then turned its cute little head and looked directly at me. The bird then flew back up towards the ceiling flying so close to the top of my head that I could feel the breeze from its flight on my face. There were many little giggles, smirks and self-contained laughter.

The minister proclaimed, "We wouldn't want to exclude any of god's creatures from taking communion!"

Then there was a moment or two of laughter and the service continued with a more cheerful and lighthearted tone. I can't help but wonder if that was the same bird that appeared at my mother's grave. It was as if somehow this bird was here to give me a message from my mother.

After communion, the minister said "Even though it's not on today's program, I think "All Things Bright and Beautiful", page 57 in your hymnal, would be a most appropriate song."

I couldn't have been more moved! The song started out, "All things bright and beautiful, all creatures great and small,

all things wise and wonderful, the Lord God loves them all." The choir chimed in and it was a magnificent experience!

On the way to Johnny's house I asked him if he would mind if I joined him and his family at church every Sunday.

When we entered Johnny's house, the wonderful aroma of home cooking filled the air. I have to admit that my father and aunt Savita's cooking leaves much to be desired. We all feasted on a delicious ham dinner with roasted potatoes, sautéed asparagus and carrot cake for dessert.nThey treated me as if I were part of the family. It was such a warm sensation of belonging. I think now that I am not only in love with Johnny, but also in love with the idea of becoming part of his family! His father also suggested that next year, perhaps my father, Aunt Savita and Raj would all like to join us for Easter dinner. At the risk of being too forward, I gladly accepted on their behalf.

March 31, 1964

I can hardly believe it! Johnny and I both had one of the top essays! I was number one! Johnny was number 9! We will be going to the World's Fair in Queens, New York on opening day, April 22nd. We will leave on the 21st and stay overnight in a hotel on the 21st and the 22nd.The theme of the fair is "Peace through Understanding." I am so jazzed!

CHAPTER FOUR
APRIL

April 1, 1964

Geez, am I ever an April fool! Johnny picked me up early for school and told me that he had to make a slight detour. We drove into a wooded area near by. Suddenly, the car came to an abrupt halt. He became frustrated and tried to start it to no avail. He told me that we must have run out of gas! He instructed me to wait in the car while he ran to get gas from the nearest gas station. I was so worried that I would be tardy for my Social Studies class which is first period. He was only gone for a few minutes when he came back. He wasn't holding a gas can but instead he had in his hands a breathtaking bouquet of freshly picked wildflowers. He handed me the bouquet, and cheerfully said, "April fools!" We then embraced and kissed for what seemed to be an endless time, but in reality, was probably all of ten seconds! He then started the car and drove to school, getting us there just in time for first period.

April 2, 1964

I decided to try to obtain as much information as possible regarding our family's history from Aunt Savita. I have asked her several times if we could sit down and discuss it. She seems to be avoiding the topic.

April 3, 1964

I overheard Aunt Savita on the phone today. She was involved in a very serious conversation, but she was speaking in a hushed tone. It was as if she wanted to keep her conversation a secret from me. Then, to my delight she called, "Sandra, your father is on the phone!"

We had a very brief but wonderful conversation. I did detect some sadness and a sense of stress in his voice. I could also tell that he was doing his best to mask it. When I asked him what was wrong, he chuckled and said, "Sandra, my dear, whatever do you mean? How could there be anything wrong when I am talking to my favorite girl in the whole wide world?"

Anyway, hearing his voice gave me almost the same warm feeling as I had had at the séance. Close to the same feeling as the first time I embraced Johnny and the feeling I got from the cardinal at my mother's grave. How I long to have my dad back home!

April 4, 1964

Today, Aunt Savita approached me and told me that she would be happy to sit down with me after school and discuss my family's history.

April 5, 1964

The school day yesterday seemed to last an eternity. But what Aunt Savita told me yesterday afternoon was well worth the wait. She explained to me that the reason she was putting off our talk was that she wanted to wait to receive my father's permission before telling me the whole story.

She said that her life changed drastically when she was a girl of ten. The year was 1933. She said that she had been a quiet, lonely little girl with no one to play with. Even then, however she had learned to use her gift of psychic power.

One morning a strong feeling came over her, a feeling that there was someone waiting for her. Someone that would change her life from sad and lonely to joyful. This feeling led her on a walk, far away from the village. She came across some caves. She heard a noise and wasn't certain what it was. It sounded a bit like an animal in pain. She was soon to discover that it was not an animal but a boy! A white boy. The boy was crying. He looked to be about six or seven. He was injured and weak. Aunt Savita helped the boy back to her village, where her father, Aaryn, who was the village doctor, helped the boy to recover. That boy's name was Nigel.

I was astounded! I asked her, "Do you mean that he was my father?" She said yes, he was.

"Recovery for Nigel was a long process. Every day we would spend hours together. Gradually, your father came out of his shell and began to speak about his parents. He said that he and his parents were on a tour of India. He said that they had come from England to India for his father's work. He said that arrows were being shot at his family from all over. He ran away and found a safe hiding place. When the arrows had stopped, he came out of hiding. His parents were both laying in the dirt filled with arrows. He tried to wake them, but they were silent and limp. He said that he saw men coming back and he hid again. The men then took his parents' bodies away. He told us that he wasn't sure how long he had been on his own, hiding in the cave, foraging for food and water. He was almost skin and bones when I found him.

"Nigel and I played every day. We became very close. My parents saw a change in me. I had come out of my shell and I had become a much more cheerful girl. I knew that my parents were concerned that the British would find out about Nigel and take him away. Nigel's skin was light and he spoke with a British accent. I was so very afraid that my parents would decide to hand him over to the British authorities.

"Looking back, I believe that my parents saw that we were good for each other, and for this reason they decided to keep him with us. When they registered him for school, they used our last name. For years they would avoid taking him anywhere that the British might be. We eventually realized that it had been hunters that had shot the arrows at Nigel's parents, mistaking them for wild animals.

"As Nigel and I grew up, when we were around the British, Nigel would pretend that he didn't know our family. We in turn would act as if we didn't know him. As soon as he was old enough, your father and I left our family behind and headed for the USA.

"Your father has spoken very little about his parents. All that I know is that his parents were British. I'm not sure if there is much more that he can tell you. He became part of our family. My parents became his parents, my grandparents became his grandparents, my cousins were his and my aunts and uncles his as well. He seemed perfectly happy and content. He gave every indication that, although the family he came from must have been of a higher social and economic class than we were, he was grateful and happy that we opened our home and our hearts to him."

Jeepers! I feel so relieved! At long last I have an explanation as to why my father's and my skin is so much lighter than that of my aunt's, and why I have not inherited the physic powers!

Now, its' time to catch some ZZs. Goodnight!

April 8, 1964

I have decided that since my father was content with considering the Chaudhry's his family, I will be content with considering them mine. Now it is time to move on to my mother's side of the family.

April 10, 1964

When I walked out the door this morning there was a huge rock on the door step with a small rock next to it. On the huge rock the word NO was painted. The small rock had the word YES. Sticking out from underneath the huge rock there was a note explaining that if I would like to accept Johnny's prom invitation, I should bring the small rock to the gate. If not, I should carry the huge rock to the gate! Well, ha-ha! Of course, I would accept Johnny's prom proposal. Even if I didn't accept, there was no possible way that I could pick up the huge rock. So, I brought the small rock to the gate where Johnny awaited me with a bouquet of one of my mother's favorite flowers (Lilies of the Valley.) I handed him the rock and he handed me the flowers. A more than fair exchange!

Johnny admitted that he realized it would be impossible for me to carry the huge rock, therefore, knowing full well that I could only say yes! I sat close to him all the way to school and he kept one arm around my shoulder as he drove. The entire drive there I had such a warm feeling of utter contentment. As if that weren't enough "No Particular Place to Go" by Chuck Berry played on the radio!

April 12, 1964

I do not remember much about my mother's parents.

They came to stay with us once when I was about the age of five. I still have the beautiful English "look at" doll that they gave me. "Look at" meant I wasn't allowed to touch or play with the doll but I must be content with just looking at it. It was a beautiful doll to look at with big blue eyes, a pouty grin and long, wavy blonde hair. It had a beautiful green silk long dress with a white lace-trimmed pinafore. The doll seemed to look right at me and watch over me as I slept. She made me feel safe as if nothing could harm me during my slumber.

My maternal grandparents would send me packages on my birthday and at Christmas. They always sent the most delicious English sweets, biscuits and shortbread. Thinking about them, I can almost taste the delightful chocolates and the sweet Turkish delight. Our American candy couldn't hold a candle to the English confections. They would also send knickknacks, jewelry and souvenirs from all over the world.

This continued long after my mother passed away. Once I became a teenager, I would only receive a card with British pounds in it at both Christmas and my birthday.

With my father in India and my maternal grandparents in England, how am I to find out my mother's family history? Perhaps I should ask my aunt for permission to telephone my grandparents. Although, I do know that overseas calls are extremely expensive. Well, I don't have many options, so I will plan on asking Aunt Savita for her permission tomorrow.

April 13, 1964

I asked Aunt Savita about telephoning my grandparents. She suggested that I write them a letter and send it air mail.

She said that it should only take a week or two to arrive and I should provide them with my telephone number and explain how important it is for them to phone me right way. She also suggested that if it came to it, perhaps I could speak with Mr. Rabin, explain the situation and request additional time to do the report. I am going to write the letter now, dear diary, before I go to bed!

April 18, 1964

This evening after we watched "Father Knows Best" Aunt Savita received a telephone call. She talked for nearly half an hour. This is very unusual for her. She generally is not the type of person to chat on the telephone. I asked her who it was. She smiled at me but she ignored the question, and instead of answering she asked me if I had all my homework completed. She said that it would take some time to explain the subject of the phone call to me. I could not hold back my curiosity. I had finished the homework that was absolutely necessary. So, I told her that my home work was completed and not to worry about how long it would take to explain it. Now, I realize that I should have studied for my trigonometry test a little more. I will have to work twice as hard tomorrow!

Anyway, Aunt Savita told me that it was the authorities on the telephone. They had suspected that the turbaned man (Mahesh) was involved in illegal activity in India. She said that the authorities offered Mahesh a plea bargain for turning in Rudra's family. They explained that, Rudra's family was also involved in illegal international trade. Apparently, Mahesh not only turned them in but he also told them the whole story of how he was here to extort money from our family. In exchange for his confession, he was given political asylum in the U.S. The remainder of his jail sentence was also suspended.

Aunt Savita was concerned that we could still be held responsible for the accident that my grandfather Aryan had with Rudra so many years ago. But the authorities assured her that there was nothing to worry about. They told her that even if it had not been an accident, we are not responsible for the sins of our fathers. They said that the participants in the illegal activity will be brought to trial in India.

Aunt Savita told me that the court date has been set for June 5th. They also said that we could most likely expect restitution for all of the past payments our family has made to Rudra's family over the years. My father will be testifying against them.

As Aunt Savita explained this to me, she seemed relieved, like she had been holding a brick above her head and she was finally allowed to drop it. When she had finished explaining all this to me, she said, "I'm off to a bath and bed!" She then ran up the stairs with energy and joy in her step, almost as if she were a teenage girl running to meet with her boyfriend.

I am so relieved that all of this worked out. I'm sure that I'll fall asleep with a smile on my face.

April 20, 1964

I am so jazzed! This trip to the World's Fair is going to be out of this world! I am all packed and ready to go. Johnny is picking me up tomorrow morning. We will go to school and then board the bus at 9:00 am!

April 21, 1964

It was late in the afternoon by the time we reached our hotel. I was assigned a room with a girl named Joann. The room had two twin beds separated by a nightstand. I tried to make conversation with Joann but she seemed shy and withdrawn. She was a pretty girl. She had medium length wavy, light brown hair with large green eyes. She had a solemn look on her face that projected feelings of introversion and resentment. She was quite a bit shorter than I. I would estimate around 5'2. While I am a whopping 5'7. Despite her solemn look, somehow, I knew that there was a nice person underneath her icy cover. There must have been something traumatic that had happened to her to make her so shy. I invited her to have dinner with Johnny and me, but she said that she already had plans to have dinner with her assigned partner, Janet.

When Janet came to the door, I was very surprised to see the stark difference between the two girls. They were like night and day! Janet was taller than even I. She was as thin as a rail. She had beautiful, long blonde hair. I had seen her around school, hanging with the popular crowd. I suspect that her popularity was in part due to her snug fitting flashy clothes. She seemed very outgoing but also, she seemed to have a bit of a sassy-pants attitude. She sashayed into our room with such confidence and with her nose raised so high that if one didn't know any better, we may have mistaken her for the princess of the 1964 World's Fair. I was a bit concerned about Joann going off alone with Janet tomorrow. I guess it's not really my place to say anything. Is it?

April 22, 1964

To say our trip to the World's Fair was out of this world would be an understatement. The first really cool thing we saw was the Unisphere, a huge globe made out of stainless steel. Next, we saw a show on the History of Communications. Then we took an outdoor elevator to the top of the highest tower of the fair. The view was amazing, as we gazed out over the fair, Johnny turned his head towards me, he put his hand under my chin and gently turned my face towards him. He then brushed my loose hair back tenderly all the while gazing into my eyes. It was so intense! He then gave me a gentle but passionate kiss. I felt as if I were the happiest girl in the world. Well, I bet that I was, at least the happiest in the World's Fair!

We saw the unveiling of a car that was the absolute MOST! It was called a Ford Mustang. Johnny vowed that someday he would own one. We sat on the floor in "Japan" and drank tea. We walked from "Asia" to "Africa" in less than ten minutes! We watched African natives dancing to drums. We went to the "Old West" where they had a player piano and Johnny tried the shooting range. He shot down every single duck! We went on an antique car ride and explored a Belgium village where we rode a beautiful carousel. We went on a ride called "Futurerama". This ride made me believe that we really will send a man to the moon someday. I think that my favorite was "The Carousel of Progress". The seats moved around an animated showcase of a family progressing into the future. The catchy tune that they sang is still in my mind: "It's a Great Big Beautiful Tomorrow."

Johnny's favorite was the Skydome Spectacular; it showcased man's effort to harness the sun's energy.

As we left the Skydome I noticed a girl sitting on a bench with her head tilted towards the ground. There was a definite similarity between her and Joann. Johnny and I approached her. As we drew closer, I was surprised to see that it was in fact Joann. We greeted her and as she looked up at us, I noticed that her eyes were moist and she immediately wiped a tear away from her cheek with her shirt sleeve. She looked as if she were ashamed that she had been crying. I feel guilty. I should have stopped her from going to the fair with Janet!

Johnny sat down on one side of her and I sat down on the other. We asked her what had happened and she replied that Janet had been flirting with some boys. One of the boys had asked Janet to go on "The Small World" ride with him.

"The other boy, Roy, and I tagged along. Janet and the boy she had been flirting with, Mike, sat in the front of the boat. Mike had his arm around Janet. Roy and I sat just behind them. Roy tried to put his arm around me and I tried to pull away, but he was persistent. Then about half way through the ride he tried to kiss me! I tried to pull away but again, but he was determined. Finally, I managed to pull away from him. I shouted out, 'You have bad breath!' and slapped his face! Just then the ride ended, I got out of the boat as quickly as possible and ran away. Well, here I am."

Johnny and I did our best to comfort Joann and cheer her up. We even told her that we would love to have her hang out with us, but she was insistent that she just wanted to go back to the hotel, take a bath and read a book. So, we walked her back to the hotel.

After we got her back to the hotel safely, we decided to go

on "It's a Small World" ourselves. It had animatronic figures from what seemed to be about one hundred different countries. They were all dressed in their native costumes and moving around, dancing and interacting with each other. All throughout the ride, the song "It's a Small World" played. I was awe struck! Some extremely talented people must have designed and created all of those beautiful dolls, costumes, and settings!

In the evening there was a spectacular fireworks show. Johnny and I enjoyed the show snuggled in a blanket that he purchased in the "Mexican Village". After that Johnny was hungry. We had only eaten snack food all day. So, we went to "Hawaii" and ate at Restaurant of the Five Volcanoes. We had a delicious dinner followed by dancing under the stars. Not even in the far-off corners of my imagination could I envision a more exciting day and a more romantic evening! We danced all night until the band stopped. I looked at my watch and it was 2:00 am! To avoid turning from Sanderella back to Sandra, I thought I had better get back to the hotel room right away! So, here I am with you, dear diary.

April 23, 1964

I am writing this on the bus; we are heading back to Boston. Johnny has fallen asleep with his head on my shoulder, making it a bit difficult to write. He really has an enormously heavy head! I guess all those brains must weigh quite a bit. He has been sleeping a lot along the way. The first time he fell asleep I was able to sneak over to Joann's seat. She was sitting alone so I thought I would try again to strike up a conversation with her. I was successful! She did open up to me a bit. She also will be attending The U in the fall. She has already decided on majoring in journalism.

She also told me that she is the youngest in her family. She was nearly in tears when she told me that her older brother was killed last year in Vietnam. I guess that I was correct about something traumatic happening in her life. Having your brother killed in Nam, or anywhere for that matter, would be enough to throw anyone for a loop!

I told her a bit about my family situation. She seemed to be genuinely intrigued. She said that she will be taking a creative writing class at the U over the summer. I told her that I would love to take a creative writing class. She said that she would bring me the registration form. We made plans to meet in the school cafeteria for lunch on Monday. I think that we really clicked! I am very hopeful that we will become close friends. It would certainly be nice to have a close girlfriend, especially once I get to college.

April 25, 1964

Everything is going peachy keen dear diary. I do have some big news. Raj announced this evening in a voice that sounded as proud as a dad boasting about his son getting into Harvard, that he and Aunt Savita have set a wedding date for Sept 16th. They said that my father expects to be home by then! I do hope that they are right. I really do miss him! Of course, Aunt Savita is never wrong when it comes to predicting the future. Aunt Savita then asked me if I would like to be her Maid of Honor. She said that Indian weddings typically don't have a Maid of Honor or Brides Maids so she not certain exactly what the position would entail. I was honored to accept anyway. I have no idea what an Indian wedding ceremony is like but I can hardly wait to find out!

There is one thing that has been a cause for concern. I had hoped to hear from my English grandparents regarding my family history. Aunt Savita assured me that I could expect to hear from them soon. There isn't much that my aunt doesn't know.

April 28, 1964

You'll never guess who I heard from! You got it! Grandma and Grandpapa Baden from England! They not only gave me enough family history to complete my report but they also invited me to come and visit them in England this summer! It looks like I may not be able to take the creative writing class with Joann after all. A more than adequate trade, I think. Don't you agree dear diary?

CHAPTER FIVE
MAY

May 1, 1964

I have a date all arranged to visit Grandma and Grand-papa in England! I can hardly wait! I will leave on June 9th. This is a few days after high school is over forever. In other words, my graduation. Next week is Prom. The theme is "Heaven on Earth." I love my life! It seems to be filled with endless celebrations!

May 2, 1964

I am so glad that I have gotten to know Joann. She has been sitting with Johnny and me at lunch every day. I have never had a close girlfriend before. Johnny and I are going to set her up with his friend, Ernie, from another high school who is also a senior. Johnny tells me that he is president of his high school debate team. The four of us are going out for burgers tomorrow night.

May 3, 1964

We had a great time on our double date. Joann and Ernie really seemed to hit it off! Johnny picked Ernie up first, then me and lastly Joann. Ernie and Joann talked almost nonstop from the time Joann sat down in the car.

Johnny went to the juke box and played "Tutti Fruity", the song we danced to at the roller rink on our first date. He asked me to dance. There wasn't exactly a dance floor but there was a clear area in front of the juke box so we tore up the floor while everyone watched. The next song was "Teenager in Love". This time Ernie and Joann joined us on our makeshift dance floor. They seem to be a perfect match.

On the way back we had to stop for gas. A guy that

Johnny knows from school whose name is Bruce was the gas station attendant. He enthusiastically ran out to us. He really seemed to be enjoying his job as he filled the Galaxy up with regular, checked the oil and wiped the windows. He then casually asked if any of us had seen Janet around. I guess he must have a thing for her. Bruce doesn't seem to be the type of guy that I would picture Janet with. He's kind of grubby, but good looking in a rough sort of way. He has long black curly hair. He was wearing torn blue jeans and a dirty white tee shirt with a pack of smokes rolled up in the sleeve. I had seen him around school, but he's not the kind of guy I would associate with. He is one of the Greasers.

Oh well. Time for bed. Good night dear diary.

May 4, 1964

It is so fab! Ernie asked Joann to Prom! Now the four of us can go together! Joann and I are going dress shopping tomorrow!

May 5, 1964

The dresses we found are absolutely gorgeous! Mine is a pink strapless, full length gown. It has lace trim at the top and the skirt is made of satin. It has a wide ribbon just above the waist. It came with silk gloves that come just above my elbows and a nifty hair piece. I felt like a true princess in the few brief moments I wore it in the shop. I believe I can wear the white heels that I already have.

Joann's gown is a similar style in a light violet color, although it does have straps and it doesn't have lace.

I can hardly wait for Saturday night!

May 8, 1964

The prom lived up to its name. It felt like heaven on earth as we danced the night away! We went out on the balcony and gazed at the stars while we discussed all our plans for the future. Johnny wants to be a doctor and I would like to write a novel. We see ourselves with four children, two cats and a dog. We agreed that we definitely need a white picket fence to complete the dream.

We saw Bruce and Janet together out on the terrace. They were necking. When Johnny and I saw them, we made a beeline right back to the dance. I don't know how they can do that in such a public place!

Joann and Ernie seemed to get along nicely. Every time that I glanced over at Joann, she was either chatting or dancing with Ernie. After the dance a lot of people went to a park they call Rubber Hill. I have no idea where that name came from. The hill consists of dirt and grass not rubber! Johnny, Joann, Ernie and I just went out for late night pie and ice cream.

May 12, 1964

Today Johnny came over. It was a surprise visit completely out of the blue. When he came to the door, he was far from his usual bright, cheerful self. Instead, he looked pale, gaunt and depressed. He looked as though he might bend over and vomit at any moment. I put my arm around him and sat with him on our loveseat in the great room. He explained to me that he had just found out that his mother was diagnosed with breast cancer. She is scheduled to have a radical mastectomy next Thursday. He said that her surgeon will be one the finest in all the world. I wasn't certain what a mastectomy was and Johnny explained that it was having both her breasts removed. A tear ran down his cheek and his eyes welled up. This was the first time I had seen Johnny cry. We talked into the night.

I hope that I cheered him up at little. I offered to come to the hospital with him and his family while his mother has the surgery. My heart goes out to Johnny. I know what it is like to lose a parent. I certainly wouldn't want that to happen to Johnny.

May 20, 1964

Yesterday was Johnny's mother's surgery. We sat there nervously as we held hands for hours. All the while his dad and sister played a card game of War. Johnny finally suggested that we go down to the hospital chapel to pray for his mother to pull through the surgery and recover quickly. We went down to a beautiful little chapel and prayed together. I had an inexplicable feeling that God was in fact listening.

Soon after we went back up to the waiting room only to find Johnny's dad and Stacey gone. With wild anticipation in our hearts we asked the nurse at the desk if she knew where they were. She gestured to a room at the end of hall. She then asked if we were family. Johnny replied that he was the son and that I was the soon to be daughter-in-law. I blushed at being called a soon to be daughter-in-law. I must admit that it did feel good to hear that Johnny already considered me part of the family. The nurse said that I was close enough to being family.

As we approached the room, the minister from Johnny's

church was just leaving. He and Johnny shook hands and then the minister embraced Johnny and said, "God be with you." He also shook my hand gently and then made his way down the hall.

When we entered his mother's room, she was lying silent and still. Her general anesthesia hadn't worn off yet. So, Johnny, Stacey and I went back to the waiting room. Johnny's dad stayed by his wife's side.

After two long hours, Johnny's dad came out to the waiting room. He looked worn out. His eyes were bloodshot as if he had been crying. Johnny squeezed my hand tightly. I couldn't help but fear the worst. Johnny's dad then looked at us. Looking beyond the redness I could see a sense of relief in his eyes. He said that all the cancer was removed and she should be waking up soon. Stacey ran into her dad's arms. Johnny shouted out," Thank you God!" We gave his dad a hug. He then asked us to take Stacey home and suggested we get some rest so we could have a productive day at school tomorrow.

May 25, 1964

It was Stacey's 10th birthday today. Johnny's mother, Roberta, is still in the hospital. After school we brought Stacey to the hospital so that her mother could be part of the celebration. We brought cake, balloons, presents, and horns to blow. Stacey loved the party. Actually, the whole family seemed to. Her mother had one of the hospital staff purchase a huge pink stuffed poodle for Stacey. I gave her a necklace. The pendant was shaped in the letters STACY. It was 18k gold. I told her that she could wear it when she is a bridesmaid in our wedding. Seeing her face all aglow when I told her made my heart sing. Johnny gave her several 45s including "I Wanna Hold Your Hand!" Her dad gave her a hula hoop and money. After singing happy birthday we all bent down over Roberta and gave each other a unified hug.

Just as we were leaving, she called out in a weak voice, "Sandra." I came back to her. She whispered to me, "I would like you to call me Mom."

I managed to get out, "I'd love to, Mom." I then softly shut the door behind me before bursting out in tears! I was so touched but at the same time a sad feeling of melancholy came over me as, I was selfishly thinking of how I miss my own mother so much.

As we walked out of the hospital, there perched on a branch was a cardinal. I am sure that it was THE cardinal. It sang its usual phrase with authority a few times and then swooped down on Stacey and grabbed a few strands of her hair in his beak. It playfully pulled the hair up above her head and then let it go. It chirped a few more times and flew back up high into the sky. There is no doubt in my mind that it was sent by my mother to wish Stacey a happy birthday, and possibly to tell me that it was okay to call Roberta "Mom".

May 30, 1964

Everything is going well dear diary. I am becoming closer friends with Joann. We went on another double date with Joann and Ernie the other night. This time we went to a drive-in movie and stayed for the whole double feature. This was my first drive-in movie. It was a lot of fun, but more because of the company, the snacks and the uniqueness of the experience than the movies themselves. It was past 1:00 am by the time we left the drive-in!

Later this evening, as my Aunt Savita and I were chatting over our turkey TV dinners (they are far from my favorite food) we reflected on the many life changing events that have occurred thus far in 1964.

CHAPTER SIX
JUNE

June 1, 1964

Johnny was chosen to be our class valedictorian! I know that he is extremely intelligent. Even with knowing that, apparently, I was still selling him short. Three more days to graduation!!

Last night was our senior party. It was really nifty. It was in a hall the PTA rented. We played games all night. Everyone, even me, won a prize. My prize was a silver bracelet that shows the year 1964 across my wrist. Joann won the grand prize which was a 19" color TV! She is certainly a lucky duck! She tells me that she intends to put it in our dorm room. So, I guess that her good fortune is also mine!

Tomorrow is the senior dinner. The day after that is our senior picnic. Then on June 5th my father is testifying in court regarding Rudra's family's claim. June 6th is our graduation day! On the 9th I leave for England. My calendar is becoming very full of excitement!

June 7, 1964

Well, graduation was incredible! If God himself had taken our order, we couldn't have had better weather. The sun was shining down on us and I felt a warm, almost supernatural glow in my heart. There was just enough of a breeze so that it wasn't too hot.

Johnny gave an amazing speech. You could hear the birds singing in between the announcements, and you'll never guess which bird was up to his usual shenanigans. Our very special cardinal of course!

Just after they announced Sandra Elizabeth Chaudhry,

everyone applauded. Then down from the sky swooped the cardinal. He landed right on top of my cap. He grabbed my tassel and proceeded to fly away, with my hat in his beak! He didn't go far before he dropped my cap right in Johnny's lap! Johnny was sitting in the 2nd row just behind Mr. Rabin. As my cardinal friend flew away with my cap the entire crowd looked up at him in astonishment. Then, when he dropped the cap in Johnny's lap there was a universal roar of laughter. I watched everyone as they threw their caps into the air and I felt as elated as their caps must have felt as they soared through the air. It certainly made for a memorable and light-hearted end to our high school years!

June 8, 1964

I had a quiet day today. I spent most of the day packing for my England trip. I am very excited, but at the same time my heart aches at the thought of leaving Johnny, Joann and Aunt Savita. The best thing that happened today was receiving a phone call from my father. He seemed so much more cheerful than the last time we spoke. He said that the trial was over and Rudra's family has been ordered to pay us a monthly restitution for the next twenty years along with an immediate lump sum distribution. He also said that he plans on returning from his sabbatical early!

June 9, 1964

I am on the airplane crossing the Atlantic Ocean as I write this dear diary. Johnny took me to the airport. It was a very romantic goodbye. Johnny wiped away the tear that rolled down my cheek after we hugged and kissed goodbye. He told me that he would be anxiously awaiting the return of his sweet wayfarer. I have never felt such sorrow parting from someone. I had thought saying goodbye to dad when he went on his sabbatical was difficult, but this was a whole other level. There are many empty seats on this flight. Enough so that I can stretch out a little bit and hopefully get some shuteye.

As I sit here, I am reminiscing about all the recent events in my and my family's life. It seems as though between the time my mother died and my seventeenth year, life was routine. Nothing extraordinarily good and nothing extraordinarily bad happened. In the past five months, however, I believe there has been more excitement than in all those past twelve years combined! Now flying to England on my own to meet my mother's parents feels very daring and exciting indeed!

June 10, 1964

So many amazing things happened yesterday dear diary! First of all, when I reached London and I walked off the plane, there waiting for me were my grandparents. But they were not alone. With them was a boy. I wondered who on earth this boy could be. His hair was very close to the same color as mine. He was tall and slender, as am I. He smiled at me with the same wide-toothed grin that I have.

My grandmother was beautiful. Her hair was completely white and she wore a loving expression that made me feel so welcomed. Her eyes were closed, and her hands were cupped over her heart. Her face was care worn. Yet when she opened her opened her eyes, they were still a deep blue and they twinkled like little bright stars as she looked at me. I could see the exuberant youth trapped within her wrinkled and aged shell. She was the first to embrace me and she did so with great enthusiasm. Her English accent flowed almost like music.

"It is so lovely to see you my darling Sandra," she said.

Next, was my Grandfather who had a serious look on his face as he gave me gentle, heartfelt hug. His hair was also pure white. Following the hug, he grinned at me, our eyes met and an undeniable feeling of kindness, compassion and love radiated from him. "I have never seen anyone so well turned out! You look so very much like your mum!"

And finally, the boy said, "Hello, Sandra, my name is Samuel. I'm very pleased to meet you." We extended our hands for a brief shake.

We took the train directly from London to Southampton. We had a lovely visit on the way. It was interesting to hear stories of my mother's childhood. I did not want to be rude, so I did not ask why this boy Samuel came with them. From Southampton, we took a taxi to a small village just a short drive away.

The driver let us off at the end of a cobblestone street. Ahead there was a scene so beautiful that it could have been a painting. There was a pretty, little, white bridge that provided a path from one side of a stream to the other. A beautiful aroma from a combination of fresh water, flowers and other foliage filled the air. You could see a clear reflection of the surrounding trees in the water. It glistened beneath the rays of sunshine as it flowed down the stream. On the opposite side of the stream there was a small hill. Perched at the top of the hill was a quaint thatched cottage. In the front of the cottage there was the most beautiful flower garden that I have ever seen! The garden encompassed the cottage with such magnificence that it defies one's imagination. There was ivy climbing all over the sides of the house as if it wanted to claim the house as its own. The entire scene seemed like it was straight out of a storybook. I absolutely love it.

A small white dog with brown spots came running towards me with the speed of a lightning bolt. As I came closer to the cottage. The little dog wagged his tail so hard it seemed it might fall off at any moment. He greeted me with so much enthusiasm that he jumped up and bumped his nose with mine. I have always wanted a dog, but whenever I asked, my father always said, "Perhaps someday," Samuel told me that the dog's name is Danny and he is sometimes a bit too friendly.

As I entered the garden, I noticed that it abounded with all of my mother's favorites: lilies of the valley, red and yellow roses, lilacs, peonies, petunias, fuchsias, and tulips. It was like a larger much more illustrious version of my mother's tribute garden back home. Vines ran purposefully up a trellis on each side of the front door to the cottage.

When we entered, the wooden floors creaked under my feet as my grandmother showed me to my room. It is a small corner room on the upstairs level directly across from Samuel's room. In the center of my room there is a large four poster bed. It seemingly called out "Collapse on me, Sandra," and I enthusiastically jumped right in! It felt like I was on a cloud! I have never been so comfortable. There are three soft as a cloud pillows and a big fluffy quilt. My gran calls it an eiderdown. She told me that she would return in a few minutes to tuck me in.

I opened the dresser drawers to put some of my clothes away and to my sheer delight one of the drawers was filled with English sweets! There was a note in the drawer that read: "Sandra, our love, please enjoy these. Grandma and Grandpapa."

As I began to put my clothes away, I was taken with the floral scent that filled the drawers. Then Gran came back momentarily. She was carrying a hot water bottle. She told me to hold it closely under my eiderdown. She said that it would keep me warm from head to toe. I asked her how she managed to have such lovely scented drawers and she told me that the drawers have sachets in them. She said that she had made them from the flowers in the garden. She told me that if I would like to learn how to make them, she would teach me.

"Good night, sleep tight, mind the fleas don't bite! I will see you in the morning light," Grandma told me. I still can't get over how beautiful her voice is. It sounds to me more like a bird singing its song than a person speaking. She then kissed me tenderly on my cheek and left, closing the door softly behind her. I felt as safe and warm as a baby kangaroo tucked in its mama's pouch.

June 11, 1964

I found out today who the boy is. The shock is still making my mind twirl! Can it be real? My grandmother explained to me that my mother died of post-partum bleeding after giving birth to Samuel. My father was so distraught that he couldn't even bring himself to hold Samuel. In his mind, if it hadn't been for Samuel, Cassandra would still be alive. She said that I was sent to stay with my parent's friends, the Dahl family, while my mother was recovering from giving birth. Apparently, I must have had a wonderful time with the Dahl family. I do recall that they had a son and a daughter close to my age. Playing with other children was such a rare treat for me that I must not have concerned myself with my mother's wellbeing. Somehow, she must have either hidden the pregnancy from me or I blocked it from my memory. Maybe I was just too young to notice.

My grandmother explained that she and Grandpapa asked my father's permission to take Samuel back to England with them while my father recuperated from his loss. Weeks grew into months; one season changed to the next and the months grew into years. He still has never come to visit. She said that subconsciously he must still blame Samuel for the death of his beloved wife.

June 15, 1964

I do love it here! I have been getting acquainted with my fun loving, adorable little brother! He has taught me how to play cricket and English football—what we call soccer. I read Mark Twain to him in the evenings. We have finished Tom Sawyer and now we are half way through Huckleberry Finn. He tells me that he is having a wonderful time with me and he would like to visit us in America someday.

I feel as if my heart has been a broken puzzle and knowing my brother has allowed me to fit in the last piece.

We have a connection that can't be denied.

Samuel also tells me that he does not hold it against our father that he hasn't come to visit. He says that he knows it must have been terribly painful to lose the love of his life. He is certainly wise and mature beyond his years.

Every morning the four of us, along with Danny the dog, walk to the beautiful and historic town of Romsey. We buy our groceries for the day.

We explore the shops and dream about all the things we would like to buy someday. It is far more exercise than I am used to and by lunch time I am ready to collapse! Lunch is our main and largest meal. Everything tastes so fresh. We will have a vegetable (my favorite is the cauliflower but the Brussels sprouts are also delicious.) We also have potatoes cooked in a variety of ways: new potatoes, fried potatoes, baked potatoes, mashed potatoes, stewed potatoes, and the best by far: cheesy potatoes. We will also have some form of meat. The lamb with mint sauce is delightful! After a delicious lunch I am energized again.

Gran and Grandpapa Baden then take their nap while Sam and I find some way to entertain ourselves. Sometimes the neighbor children of various ages come out and we'll all go to the park, which is just a short walk, and we usually play blind man's bluff, freeze tag or red-light green- light—no rough stuff. There are five-year-old's all the way through six-teen-year olds. I do believe that I am the oldest "child". I don't mind a bit though. It gives me a chance to feel like a kid again. I am savoring one last bit of childhood before I enter the world of a young adults. At times I have felt that I am like Patty on *The Patty Duke Show*. Then again, especially since I've been here, I feel that I am more like Patty's identical cousin Cathy.

When Gran and Grandpapa are up from their nap, Sam

and I clean up and Gran makes a lovely and elegant "tea" around 4pm. We drink tea from delicate china tea cups. We always have a delicious array of biscuits, cakes, and little sandwiches with the crust cut off. We use cloth napkins and put on our very best manners. I feel as though I'm royalty. Then Sam and I clean up the dishes. I must say that Sam has the best manners that I have ever observed in a boy.

Dinner is a snack with hot coco to drink, not a big full meal like we have in the States. I feel so well taken care of and even spoiled. If this is what a normal childhood is like, I feel as if I really did miss out! When I have kids of my own, I will do my best to make sure that this is the sort of childhood that they are given!

June 18, 1964

Today we took a cab and went to visit another nearby town to go shopping.

Our first stop was a pet shop. As I entered the shop, I heard an odd voice. In a very British accent, it said "Hello, have a look round." The only person I could see was girl who looked to be close to my age standing behind the counter. Soon, I heard it again, "Hello, have a look round." The girl smiled at me and gestured to a large green parrot sitting on a perch next to the counter! I then realized that it was this delight-ful bird speaking to me in a British accent! I'm not sure why it seems so odd for a bird to have a British accent. It only makes sense, right? The parrot's name was Polly and she had quite a large vocabulary. Gran, Grandpapa, Sam and I all had a lovely time talking to Polly and listening to her request crackers and repeat nearly everything we said.

In the back of the shop there were three adorable little puppies. I played with the fluffy little fur balls through the bars of their cages. How I would love to take one home, but I guess that will have to wait until Johnny and I have a home of our own.

June 20, 1964

It has been lovely bonding with Sam and my grandparents. To think that all these years we could have known and enjoyed each other. If only my father could have handled it better. I am so proud of my little brother. He is big enough not to blame our father. I suppose that I should try to be that big as well. I am so delighted to have discovered my long-lost family members!

June 28, 1964

I have been having a marvelous time. Gran, Gramps, Sam and I all went sightseeing in London for four days. London is out of this world! We saw Big Ben, Buckingham Palace, The Cutty Sark, and Westminster Cathedral. We went to the British Museum. It is mind blowing to see how old so many things are in England. In Boston, we marvel at something if it is a couple of hundred years old. In England, many things are a couple of thousand years old! We stood with one leg on each side of the Prime Meridian Line. It divides the east and west hemispheres. We saw the Beefeaters in their colorful uniforms, the marvelous Crown Jewels, and The Tower of London. We climbed up the tower. There was an extremely steep and winding stair case. With each step I climbed I felt as if I was moving one step further back in time, until finally we reached the top. Apparently, it is nicknamed 'the bloody tower' because twelve-year-old Prince Edward V and his little brother were said to have been murdered by their power-hungry uncle while being held captive there.

Sam and I rode in the upper level of a double-decker bus while Gran and Gramps sat below. Sam insisted that we sit in the very front row. He said that his friends had told him how cool it was. As we turned corners, I was sure that we were going to run right into light posts, trees and buildings! What an exciting time!

We ate the most delicious Chinese and Italian food that I have ever tasted! We had the best fish and chips! They were much better than the fish and chips in Boston! I think that this is at least in part is because here they don't use ketchup on French fries, (or as the English call them, chips), but they use malted vinegar instead.

We went to an amazing wax museum. It was unbelievable how life like all the wax statues were. As we entered there was a man taking tickets, and when Grandpapa handed the man our tickets, we all chuckled when we realized the ticket taker was in fact a wax statue! There were figures of many important political figures, royalty and movie stars.

Down in the basement they had a dungeon of horrors. Next to Salem it is the creepiest place I have ever set foot in. It was cold, dark and gloomy. A musty smell filled the air. I felt like a mouse in a maze desperately searching for an exit. At every turn there were terrifying wax figures of infamous criminals. Many of them were behind bars. As I made my way through as quickly as possible, I bumped into a wax figure of Jack the Ripper. He stood there with a bloody knife in his hand. As I stopped and read the sign, chills went up and down my spine. It said that he was a London murderer of women from the 1800's. It was SOOO creepy! I could feel my heart beat faster, as I looked back at Samuel, I saw a look of sheer terror that filled his face. He looked like a frightened bunny rabbit that stopped dead in its tracks. I grabbed Sam's hand, pulled him toward the exit and made a mad dash out the door! I am hoping that I don't have night- mares tonight, but I probably will!

June 29, 1964

I did wake up in a startled state in the middle of the night last night. I had been dreaming about running away from Jack the Ripper. He had a knife in his hand and was about to stab me when I let out a scream so loud that it woke me up in a panic. Grandpapa Will heard me scream and came in to check on me. I soon caught my breath and calmed down.

Grandpapa and I had a long, in depth chat. It is wonderful to get to know my grandfather. I feel much closer to him now. I found out that his full name is William Robert Samuel Baden. I have never known anyone with four names before! He explained to me that his father, my great grandfather, was a Lord and my great grandmother a Lady. Grandpapa Will grew up on a large estate with many servants. His older brother, my Great Uncle Harold, inherited the estate and was handed down the title of Lord. He was married but has no children and his wife is deceased. He said that he is estranged from his brother and they haven't spoken for many years.

June 30, 1964

I received a phone call today. It was my father! He told me that all is well and that on his way home from India he will come and visit all of us. We can then fly back to the States together! I have never heard a more cheerful tone in his voice! It must feel so wonderful for him to be free from the awful Rudra penance! He will also be meeting his son for the first time since he was a newborn babe. I am going to pray that their meeting will result in a permanent reunification.

CHAPTER SEVEN
JULY

July 2, 1964

Although I am having a wonderful time here and I feel much loved, my thoughts are turning more and more frequently to Johnny. I have received only one letter from him. I'm concerned about how his mother is doing. His letter to me was short and I could sense that he was masking pain behind his pen. I am considering, although I know that it would be expensive, asking Gran and Grandpapa if I could call Johnny. I really feel that I could cheer him up, if given the opportunity. I also made it known to Gran and Grandpapa how much I would like to meet my Great Uncle Harold Baden.

July 4, 1964

Well, there is no fireworks celebration here for the fourth. As a matter of fact, I have even overheard some of the English children call me a "Yank!" It bothered me a bit mostly because to me a Yankee is a player on our rival baseball team.

I didn't need to ask Gran and Grandpapa if I could call Johnny after all. Johnny's heart and mind must be synchronized with mine, like a car is with its key. He called me today!

It was a bitter sweet phone call. We professed our love and how much we miss each other. He told me how his heart ached for me and he told me a little about the difficult time his mother is having with the chemotherapy. Johnny said that he and Stacey have been doing most of the cooking, housekeeping and caring for their mother while she is sick. Their dad also hired a nurse to come in part time to help out. He said that he would like nothing more than to visit me in England but that he is very much needed at home right now.

Johnny is not one to complain but he did say that it is very difficult to watch his mother suffer. My heart goes out to him. I wish that there was something I could do to help.

When I asked him if there was anything I could do to help, he simply replied, "Hearing your voice and knowing that I will soon be able to hold you in my arms is help enough. But Sandra, if you could pray for her to get through this with a minimum amount of suffering, I bet that God would listen to you."

His voice was quiet and muffled as if he was fighting the urge to cry. I felt so helpless and my stomach felt like I just ate a batch of sour grapes. I went up to my room and spent a good hour sobbing, praying, thinking about how much I miss Johnny, and worrying about what he must be going through. My solace was interrupted when Sam knocked on the door and asked me if everything was okay. Without any hesitation, I opened the door. I was slightly embarrassed to have him see me in such a miserable state. I told him everything as my tears continued to flow. Sharing my misery with him did give me some relief.

Sam's maturity never ceases to amaze me. Soon there was another knock. It was Gran and Grandpapa. They listened to me somberly and reverently, as if every word I said was being spoken on the wireless by Prime Minister Churchill during WWII. Grandpapa told me that God would take care of Johnny and his family and that I would be back with Johnny soon. He also said that he thinks that once Johnny and I are together again, the overwhelming joy of being together will make up for the time apart. I told them that I don't know what I ever did to deserve such wonderful Grandparents and such an amazing little brother!

July 8, 1964

Well, I received quite a surprise yesterday. Grandpapa Will made an announcement. He said he received a telegram stating that his older, estranged brother Harold is in failing health. He has requested a visit with Grandpapa and any additional family members that would be interested in visiting. Grandpapa suggested that both Sam and I come along.

July 11, 1964

It was an absolutely incredible day! We drove to Great Uncle Harold's Estate. It seemed like a long drive. Gran and Grandpapa do not own a car, so their good friends the Parson's drove us. The Parsons are a retired couple who look to be perhaps ten or so years younger than Gran and Grandpapa. The car they have seems as though it is a relic left over from WWII. It was comfortable though, with plenty of leg room.

The English countryside is beyond beautiful. We passed through many picturesque villages whose streets were lined with brick row houses, quaint little cottages, churches, shops, schools, and pubs. Every house no matter the size had a flower garden in front. Perhaps that is why the British call their yards gardens.

We stopped at a pub for lunch. It was a large, beautiful thatched roof building with small mullioned windows that were cloudy with age. Outside hung a sign with the name "Fox and Hounds." Inside the air was thick and filled with the smell of food, beer and smoke. I wondered to myself if this was an appropriate place for children. I was especially concerned for Sam. After all, despite his maturity he is nearly six years my junior. I was so surprised when Grandpapa ordered Sam a pint of beer or ale as the British call it. I had to stop myself from shouting out, "He's too young for that!" I did manage to hold back, putting my protective big sister side away. Also considering that we are in a different country with different laws.

I ordered lamb and an orange fizzy (soda). It was sumptuous! So much so that I blurted out, "Would it be possible to come here back again before I leave?"

Grandpapa said, "I believe we may be able to arrange that," while he glanced over at Mr. Parsons.

Mr. Parsons then replied, "Of course. I love a nice drive in the country and your company makes it an exceptional experience."

Gran told us over lunch that Grandpapa and Mr. Parsons were both Spit Fire pilots in WWII. She said that they shared many adventures and a very special bond. That prompted Grandpapa and Mr. Parsons to begin conversing. Grandpapa began by asking Mr. Parson "how have you been old bean?" and giving him a pat on the back. The rest of us were left out of their conversation, but they were obviously enjoying themselves. They went on and on, as if they were two best friends that hadn't seen each other in many years.

We finally arrived at Uncle Harold's gated estate. We had to press a button and announce ourselves before we were let in. As the gate opened and we drove in, I was awed by the enormity and beauty of the estate. There was a wonderful flower garden in front that had the same flowers as my mother's garden back home. Although, you could see that it was much better attended to and about ten times the size. A butler greeted us at the door wearing a black tuxedo and white gloves. It was just like you see in the old-time movies.

The entry of the house was enormous! The floor was covered in beautiful marble tile that made it gleam. A large painting of a gallant-looking young man, dressed up the dull grey walls. I sat in a chair that was in the entry. It was more of a throne, really. It had a high back and the frame was a shiny gold color. The cushion was a soft red velvet. The house had a musty odor, the smell of antiques. It was dimly lit, and as I sat there on my throne, a familiar tinge of déjà vu came over me.

The butler went upstairs and came down shortly. He told us that Lord Baden should be able to see us soon, and then invited us into the parlor for afternoon tea.

I couldn't believe my eyes! The butler brought out tray after tray of the most delectable sweets, tarts, little sandwiches, and fruits that I have ever seen! I thought that Sam's eyes would burst right out of his head. He was so elated!

We were busy indulging ourselves with the most delightful tea and sweets known to man, when an older gentleman with a white coat and a stethoscope entered the room. He introduced himself as Dr. Head. He told us that our uncle has coronary heart disease. He has suffered two small heart attacks in the past five months. He said that Lord Baden is very weak and that he would estimate that he has anywhere between three weeks and three months to live. He also said that we could visit with him now, but he recommends limiting our visits to ½ an hour.

"Lord Baden needs to avoid any stress" he said in a condescending tone. It sounded as if he were warning a small child not to touch a breakable antique.

We followed James the butler up the winding staircase. It reminded me of the staircase I had seen in pictures of the Titanic. When we entered his bed chamber there was an odd smell that filled the room. It was far from a pleasant odor, but it was unique. Perhaps it was the smell of medicines and terminal illness.

Uncle Harold was propped up in bed with his eyes shut. He had a dark wood four post bed with gold curtains drawn back on two sides. We entered the room quietly and there was a chair for each of us. Uncle Harold must have sensed our presence because just a few seconds after everyone was seated, he opened his eyes. He had a startled look on his face. The startled look soon turned into a smile. Uncle Harold shouted the word, "Brother!" He cried out with the vigor and enthusiasm of a boy calling out joyfully to his dog who had been lost and finally found. Grandpapa bent over him. He took both of Uncle Harold's hands and held them. He then he gave Uncle Harold a warm embrace. I saw a tear run down Grandpapa's cheek. Soon I realized that there were several tears running down my own cheek.

In a weak voice Uncle Harold explained that he regrets not reaching out to Grandpapa years ago. He also said that since he has been ill, he has spent much time contemplating the way Grandpapa must have felt when the entire estate was left to him, with the sole explanation that he was the eldest brother. Uncle Harold said that he likely would have felt just the same way had he been the younger brother. All these years he didn't realize what a privilege it was to inherit the estate. He took it for granted and considered it more of a responsibility, even a burden. He would have much preferred freedom like Grandpapa had. But of course, he said the grass is always greener on the other side of the fence. He said that he has gone through tough times and the estate almost went bankrupt. He said that he reduced the staff to a footman, a maid, a cook, and a gardener. He also said that he has been leasing out most of the land to local farmers.

Grandpapa then introduced Gran, Sam and I to Uncle Harold. Gran just gave his right hand a squeeze. I hesitated for a moment because I wasn't sure if I should do the same. I was relieved when he finally extended his hand out. So, we shook hands and Sam followed my lead.

Uncle Harold then said that he would like to try to make amends any way that he can and that he is open to suggestions. He said that his life on earth is coming to an end soon and he would like to leave the estate to Grandpapa Will. Grandpapa told Uncle Harold that it was too late for that. Grandpapa said that at his age he is looking for simplicity and less responsibility. Grandpapa said that it would bring him great joy if the estate was left to Samuel and Sandra. I was absolutely shocked! My mouth felt dry and a lump welled up that felt like a gigantic jaw breaker was stuck in my throat.

Uncle Harold said that he had anticipated that Grandpapa would feel that way. He said that he had taken the liberty of discussing it with his solicitors, and due to the fact that Sandra is eighteen now, she can be left the estate. He said that William can live in and care for it if he wishes or

Sandra could hire someone to do so. When Sam is eighteen, fifty percent of the estate will be transferred to him. We all gave Uncle Harold hugs before we left the room.

Then like carefree children avoiding responsibility, Sam and I ran outside. We gleefully explored the grounds of the marvelous estate that would someday be ours!

Gran had put an order in with the cook requesting lamb for dinner. The food was absolutely delectable! Prior to this, dinner at the pub was the best thing I had ever tasted. This dinner exceeded that by tenfold. The lamb seemed to melt in my mouth. We had tiny little new potatoes seasoned and cooked to perfection, asparagus smothered in something called béarnaise sauce, and to top it all off an orange fizzy to drink! The joke at the dinner table was that there would be no need to revisit Fox and Hounds after a dinner like this one. Oh, and how could I forget the bread pudding dessert? It was so delicious that I found myself hoping that we could stay the night and indulge in breakfast tomorrow morning.

Shortly after dinner, Grandpapa told Sam and me that he is a bit overwhelmed with all the news. Also, that we have been invited to spend the night. He recommends that we do so. This, he said will give us time to digest the news and we can discuss it further in the morning.

July 14, 1964

Well, dear diary, it looks as though I will soon be the proud owner of an enormous English estate! This is all so unreal! I am a bit overwhelmed at the thought of all the responsibility at such a young age. After all, I am a mere girl of eighteen. Although wasn't Queen Victoria put in charge of running the country at age eighteen? Grandpapa Will has told me not to concern myself with it now. He said that he will take care of the estate until Sam is old enough. I need only be involved to the extent that I wish to. I couldn't hope for more than that, right, dear diary?

Sam will be back in school in three days! I had thought Sam was on summer break, but apparently, he had taken time off school just because I was coming. His official summer break doesn't start until the end of July. I am not sure what I will do with myself during the days while he is at school.

July 15, 1964

My mind has been traveling home lately. I received a letter from Joann. She said that she has been doing fine. She wanted to let me know that she and Ernie are now engaged, but like us they are planning to wait until after college to get married. She said that she and Ernie have been spending a lot of time with Johnny. Joann said she often goes to his house and babysits Stacey while Ernie and Johnny go out. She said that if they didn't do that, she fears that Johnny would never get out of the house. She also said that Johnny misses me terribly. She said that the most common topic of discussion is planning all the fun things that the four of us will do when I get back home.

Oh, and she said that Janet became pregnant and that the father is Bruce. Apparently, when Janet told Bruce of the news, he told her he would pay for an abortion! When Janet told him that she didn't want to have an abortion, Bruce stopped calling and she hasn't heard from him since.

Janet, being a good Catholic girl, couldn't bear the

thought of an abortion. To her it would be murder. So, she told her parents about the pregnancy. Her parents then sent her away to a convent. Their family's hope is that they can hide the fact that she was ever pregnant. Janet will have the baby while she is away and then she will give it up for adoption. When she gets home it will be as if nothing happened and she can go on with her life as usual. Hopefully, attending college and finding a suitable husband soon.

July 18, 1964

The days are much quieter with Sam and the neighborhood kids at school all day. I have to admit the first couple of days I rather enjoyed the peacefulness and having Gran and Grandpapa all to myself. I have spent hours catching up on my letter writing. I wrote to Dad, Johnny, Aunt Savita, and Joann. I had long and interesting talks with Gran and Grandpapa. I learned all about our family history in great detail. Mr. Rabin had given me an A- on my family history report. But if I had all this information when I did the report, I'm sure I would have received an A+!

July 19, 1964

My father rang up today. He has finished his sabbatical! I am so excited that if I were a bubble, I'm sure that I would burst! Father will be stopping here this coming Friday and spending the weekend! He will see his son for the first time since Samuel was a newborn!

July 21, 1964

Father is coming tomorrow. We will meet him at the Southampton train station. The Parsons will drive all of us there, but father, Samuel and I will ride home in a cab, as it would be too crowded for all of us to fit into the Parsons car. My heart is filled with anticipation! What will it be like to have our family of three together for the first time? Of course, my own excitement must pale in comparison to Samuel's. I can only imagine his excitement and anticipation. I think that Samuel may also be a bit nervous. He is so quiet today. Without his energy surging though our house like an electrical current, it's so quiet that I can hear the floor boards creaking.

July 23, 1964

We picked father up yesterday. My heart was in my mouth as we waited for his train. The moment he stepped off of the train our eyes met and we ran into each other's arms. With the exception of when I was a little girl, this is the first and only time I recall embracing my father. It has been long overdue! It felt so good that I didn't want to leave him go. Too quickly his attention turned to Gran, Grandpapa and Samuel.

"You must be Samuel, it's a pleasure to make your acquaintance." My father said as he extended his hand to shake Sam's.

Sam did shake his hand but soon after he put both his arms around father and squeezed tightly. Father looked at me and gave me a slight smile as he returned the hug. Soon my father's face turned to a slightly red color and a tear rolled down his cheek.

He sounded as if he was man speaking his last words before death as he managed to choke out the words, "I'm so sorry I haven't been there for you."

Samuel merely said, "Please don't give it a second thought, Father. You are here now and that's all that matters." Samuel was so wise and kind beyond his years that he reminded me a bit of Tiny Tim in *A Christmas Carol*.

Father came back home with us for dinner. After dinner he excused himself and came back with gifts wrapped in newspaper. He gave all of us gifts from India. He brought Sam a set of ebony hand carved elephants with ivory tusks. He gave Grandpapa a really amazing model of the Taj Mahal. He gave Grandmother a beautiful necklace with hand crafted beads, and he gave me a large beautiful "look at" doll. She was dressed in a striking red dress trimmed in gold and she was wearing a sari. Father said it was an Indian wedding dress. I vowed to treasure the doll forever.

I wonder if Aunt Savita will wear a similar dress at her wedding.

I would imagine the warmth in our home today could be felt into the next village! We ate, talked, sang and played charades. During the festivities I glanced out the window and spotted a cardinal on a tree branch near the window. I had an inkling that it could be my cardinal friend so I opened the window. There were no screens on the window, so my cardinal friend flew right over and perched itself on the windowsill. Its tail was outside but the rest of the little bird was in the house! It chirped away with abundant exuberance and enthusiasm. We all stopped and marveled at this spirited little creature. I was amazed, could this bird have followed me all the way across the Atlantic Ocean? Eventually, the bird flew away and disappeared into the evening sky. We all looked at each other with astonishment on our faces for a few moments and then as if nothing unusual had happened we resumed our fun and games.

July 24, 1964

I have agreed to go home with father on Wednesday. I have forty-eight hours to say my goodbyes and pack up. I will feel as if part of me is missing when I leave Sam and Gran and Grandpapa, but they assured me that they will come and stay with us for a week in America. They said that they will try to plan their trip around Aunt Savita's and Raj's wedding. I can hardly believe that in only a couple of months Aunt Savita and Raj will be husband and wife and that I will be a college student!

July 26, 1964

I am writing now as I fly over the pond. Saying good bye to Sam, Gran and Grandpapa reminded me of Dorothy saying good bye in the land of Oz, minus the ruby slippers. I told Sam half-jokingly, "And Sam, I think I'll miss you most of all!" There was no shortage of emotion. I'm very glad that I had my hankie handy!

Oh, my! I must go! Oh no! *TURBULENCE!!!*

July 27, 1964

Well, after our turbulent journey, we finally landed safely. On the car ride home from the airport, as I peered through the window, everything seemed so new and modern. I was in awe as we passed two stunning, new, modern, brown brick buildings. Their windows had dark tinted glass.

Everything seems so huge here. I feel like my room is big

enough for three. My bathroom is so modern and luxurious and it is just for me! I feel as though I have gone through a time warp and I have traveled from 1940 to the present day. As much as I enjoyed the trip, it is certainly good to be back home!

The best part, of course, was seeing Johnny today. I called him to let him know that I was home. In a matter of a few minutes he was at the door. I opened the door and we fell into each other's arms. We held each other tight. The warmth and security I felt holding him was far beyond compare. Then Johnny and I engaged in the most heartfelt passionate kiss that I have ever experienced. It was a real humdinger. I tingled from my head to my toes! Now, I am sure I know what love is!

July 30, 1964

It is so good to be back. I'm glad I am here now, to support Johnny and his family. Aunt Savita and I make double portions of food almost every night and I bring dinner over to Johnny's house. Occasionally, I join them for dinner and sometimes Johnny comes over and has dinner with Aunt Savita, Raj, Father and me. It has been a great experience for me to go from a somewhat lonely child with just my father and me, to seemingly having a family of eight! I think that I can safely say that my lonely days are gone!

Tonight, Johnny is coming to our house for dinner and then we are going on a double date with Joann and Ernie. We are going to the cinema to see a Beatles movie called *A Hard Day's Night.*

CHAPTER EIGHT
AUGUST

August 1, 1964

A Hard Day's Night was a really groovy movie!

Aunt Savita and Raj have finally set a wedding date. They will be married at the house in mother's tribute garden on September 19th. It will be on a Saturday so that I can come from college for the wedding. We are hoping that Sam and Gran and Grandpapa will come. I would so love for them to meet Johnny!

I am also hoping that I will receive my room assignment soon. I am so excited to go to college! Joann and I made a request to room together. I am keeping my fingers crossed!

August 3, 1964

Johnny's mother took a turn for the worse last night. She is in the hospital with double pneumonia. This is especially serious because of her now compromised immune system.

August 4, 1964

I spent all last night in the hospital with Johnny, Stacey and Johnny's dad, George. Johnny and I spent most of the time in the waiting room, the chapel and the cafeteria. Johnny's dad was in the room with Johnny's mom all night. At last George came out of Roberta's room. It was about 7:00 am. His hair was mussed, his strong face looked like a deflated balloon and his eyes were sunken and red. He sat down, collapsing like a tent being blown over in a wind storm.

He let out a deep sigh and put his arm around Stacey. "She has pulled through and she would like to see all of you."

Johnny had his arm around me. I could feel the tension leave his body and then I felt mine release also. We turned to each other and each managed an ever so slight grin.

When we entered Roberta's room, we were surprised to see that she was sitting up. Her eyes were bright and she was smiling. We gathered around her. Her first words were concern for our wellbeing.

"When was the last time you kids had a meal?" She spoke in a quiet voice, and I thought to myself, *what a kind and unselfish woman she is!*

Johnny, Stacey and I left the hospital feeling confident that Roberta would make a full recovery. As we left, sure as the snow will fly in December there was our friendly cardinal singing away. It was perched on a narrow branch of a large oak tree. A feeling of comfort and joy swept through me and left me with a delightful afterglow.

I feel as though we were all truly blessed today.

August 6, 1964

I received my room assignment today. Thank you, Lord, Joann will be my roommate! I think that I am ready for college now. All of the apprehension and fear I had about starting college has now been completely resolved.

August 8, 1964

We received a telephone call from Gran, Grandpapa and Samuel today. They will definitely be coming to Boston and staying at the house for a week. They will be here to visit and for Aunt Savita's and Raj's wedding!

August 10, 1964

I went over to Johnny's today. Everyone seemed unusually cheerful. Stacey had her record player outside on the door step and she was hula hooping to "Jeepers Creepers" by Haley Mills. As Johnny and I walked in, his mother and father were there. Their faces were all aglow as if an angelic light was inside of them. They told us that they have good news to share with us. His parents announced that they had just received a call from the oncologist and Roberta's cancer is officially in remission! Roberta fell into Johnny's arms, then George surrounded both of them with a hug and waved his hand signaling me to join in. I did just that. As I was enveloped in their blanket of warmth, I wept a tear of jubilation. I felt as if a boulder that had been crushing the air from my lungs was miraculously lifted.

It is so wonderful that Johnny will be able to begin college without this sad burden to bear. It is only 10 days before we can begin moving things into our dorm room! Also, Johnny and Ernie are going to be roomies! How cool is that!

August 12, 1964

We received a call from Gran and Grandpapa today. Apparently, Uncle Harold passed away peacefully last night. Thankfully, the doctor contacted Grandpapa the day before yesterday to let him know that uncle Harold was near the end. Gran, Grandpapa and Samuel rushed over so that they were at his bedside when he passed. The funeral will be next Tuesday. Grandpapa's voice was trembling as he managed to utter that he would like me to come if at all possible.

August 13, 1964

Johnny and I are going to England! I wish that it was under happier circumstances. I feel that I should be sad. After
all we are going to attend a relative's funeral. I do have to admit, however, inside I am filled with anticipation. How can I not
be somewhat excited to be going on a trip like this with the
love of my life by my side? Johnny has been through so much
stress and sadness with his family. I really feel that this trip
will be good for him.

August 15, 1964

We are leaving for England tomorrow. Father is coming
as well. We are staying for a week and we are planning to take
some day trips. We will invite Samuel to come along on the
day trips.

August 16, 1964

I feel so blessed. Sometimes life can seem so unreal.
Here I sit, crossing the Atlantic Ocean. On one side of me is
the man of my past and on the other side of me is the man of
my future. They are both sound asleep. I am having a difficult
time keeping my eyes open as well. I will see you on the other
side of the Atlantic!

August 18, 1964

We arrived in London only two days ago. After an ex-
hausting journey we finally arrived at Great Uncle Harold's
estate. Johnny and Samuel have made fast friends. It
warms my heart to see that they are out there with father
playing their own compromise between cricket and baseball
as I write.

The funeral will be on the twenty-first. Uncle Harold was very organized. There is a guest list which includes the names of many Lords and Ladies. His funeral will be held at the largest church in all of Southampton. Gran and I are going to London for the day tomorrow. She is very adamant that we buy new outfits for the funeral. I must admit that the thought of going to a fine dress shop in London is very exciting.

August 20, 1964

I have fallen in love with being treated as a member of the upper crust! Our day in London was amazing! Grandpapa, Johnny and Sam came along as well. They went shopping for new suits. We went to the poshest dress shop that I have ever had the pleasure of being in. The shop smelled of roses and lilacs. There was tea, cookies and pastries brought to us on a silver platter as we watched dresses being modeled for us. They were the most beautiful dresses that I have ever seen. Uncle Harold had money set aside for the funeral. Our dresses and the suits will be paid for out of those funds.

Of course, I chose a black dress. It is knee length and very fitted. I also purchased a black veil. There were some alterations to be made, but they said they would have them done that same afternoon. Gran is going to give me one of her pearl necklaces. The store employees said I look like a younger version of Jackie Kennedy. Although, they said that I seem much more cheerful than Jackie looked at John's funeral.

After our dresses were purchased, we met the guys at a fabulous Italian restaurant. It was so very authentic. I ordered baked spaghetti. Its taste was off the charts! We also had bread dipped in olive oil. My tummy said, Yummy! Yummy! Yummy!

August 21, 1964

The funeral is over. One of Uncle Harold's long-time friends, Lord Ellsworth, delivered a very thoughtful and complimentary eulogy. He ended it by saying, "Some of us will be sorrowful because he is gone but I choose to be joyful because he lived."

I thought the whole event was amazing! The attendance was far greater than anticipated. People came from Norway, France, Belgium, Germany, and Austria. Apparently during World War II, Uncle Harold used his home as a place to house children. This was mainly to get them away from all the bombing in London, but he also housed orphaned refugee children. Many of those children, now adults, showed up to pay their respects. I am so proud to be his great niece.

August 22, 1964

Today father rented a car. Johnny, Sam, father and I all went on a drive to a place called The New Forest. It was a beautiful place with lots of wildlife. At one point we saw some donkeys. They came right up to our car and one of them stuck its head in the window!

The best part was the bonding that took place. Sam had all kinds of questions about his mother. Father answered all of his questions patiently and in great detail. I too, was interested to hear things about mum that I never knew.

On the way home we all sang songs. From old English folk songs to modern rock songs. It was a smashingly good time!

August 23, 1964

I am crossing the Atlantic, sitting again between the man of my past and the man of my future. At this very moment, I feel as if I am frozen in time. Here I am on the verge of adulthood. Soon, I will be entering college and leaving my childhood behind. In the brief time that I was in England I learned so much. I feel as if I am now so much older and wiser. A woman of the world! Even so, I have doubts that I am ready to be on my own. I will forever treasure this moment, for I feel so secure, between these two men who both love me, and I them. Frozen in time, somewhere over the Atlantic Ocean, at the end of the summer of my youth.

August 24, 1964

Yesterday, when I arrived home and entered my bedroom, there was a package awaiting me on my desk. It was wrapped in brown paper with string. The stamps were US stamps and the post mark was from the main Boston post office. The strange thing was that there was no return address.

I was very curious and tore off the brown paper wrapping as quickly as a seven-year-old opening the first present under the tree on Christmas morning. There it was, the most beautiful music box I have ever seen! On the lid there was a painting of a beautiful vibrant red cardinal perched on a snow-covered tree branch. There was a poem printed next to the bird.

"No matter what you do, how grown up you become, I am always with you, you and I are like one."

My hand trembled with anticipation as I opened the box.

I wound the key to the very end. To my delight beautiful music filled my senses. I bet that you can guess what song it played dear diary. That's right! "Early One Morning!" I felt a tear roll down my cheek. My throat swelled, and if I had wanted to speak, I couldn't have. A few moments later I heard Aunt Savita ask me if I had opened the package. I managed to squeak out a faint, "Yes."

I gathered myself together and went downstairs. I asked Aunt Savita if she had any idea where the package came from. She told me that it was on the door step three days ago. She just assumed that it came in the mail. She also told me that there was a beautiful cardinal sitting on the gate when she went and fetched the package. She said that the bird was very unusual in that she came very close to it and it did not fly away.

Is it possible that the music box is somehow a gift from my mother, or is this a joke being played on me? Who would be so cruel as to play a joke like this on me? I choose to believe that this is from my mother. A positive loving message that she is looking out for me. I'm sure that Johnny would agree with me. I think that I will share the news with him and only him. He has been with me many times when our friendly cardinal has shown up.

Tomorrow Johnny is coming over at 9:00 am to help me move into my dorm room.

August 26, 1964

I told Johnny about the music box and he agrees that it must be a message from my mother, though neither of us can understand how that's possible. Sometimes you just have to have faith.

We worked at moving, furiously, all day long and I am now all moved into my dorm. When we first looked at my room, I think that Johnny's and my jaws both dropped. It is so tiny compared to my room at home. Joann was sitting on the bottom bunk bed. When she first saw us, she asked us what was wrong. I suppose that she noticed our shock. The size is going to take some getting used to.

There are wooden bunk beds on the north wall and two small desks with a small chair each under a west facing window. Joann's new color TV was on top of the double dresser. The dresser is a nice size but it consumes the entire south wall. The door when left opened covers the small closet, which is just a recess in the wall with a closet rod and no door. I hope that moving in here isn't a mistake and that I will be content sharing these cozy quarters.

While I was there several girls came and introduced themselves. They all seemed very intelligent, confident and outgoing. I guess it is time to move on. I can't remain stagnant and let life pass me by. The dorm girls have already invited Joann and me to an introduction party this Saturday night.

CHAPTER NINE
SEPTEMBER

September 15, 1964

I'm sorry dear diary. My life has been so busy and so exciting that I'm afraid that I have been neglecting you. Between classes, studying, parties, and seeing Johnny at least one day a week I have not had time for you. My hope is that you will forgive me, but when I go back to college on Monday, I am going to leave you behind for safe keeping. Please don't worry I will keep you under lock and key. You will be safe here.

It is two days until the big day. Raj and Savita will be married. Tomorrow, Samuel, Gran and Grandpapa will come and spend a fortnight here. That's fourteen days. I wish that I could take time out of school to be with them, but now that I am in college there are no excuses for missing class. At least I will have the day with them tomorrow, and sometime over the following two weekends.

September 17, 1964

Our house looked more festive than I have ever seen it. The decorations were gold, black and red. Balloons, crepe paper, flowers, and wrapped presents filled the house.

The wedding was absolutely breathtaking. Aunt Savita was beautiful! Her dress was a vibrant red with gold trim. She had gold dangling earrings and a gold hairpiece with a large red stone and golden jewels that hung down on her forehead.

The aroma of curry filled the house.

The ceremony took place in our backyard, which was even more spectacular. It was a perfect day for a wedding, mid-seventies with the crispness of an autumn breeze and the sun gleaming down on the bride and groom. It was as if God himself was giving his full approval.

My father performed the ceremony. It was conducted around a huge bonfire. It seemed that they tried to bring many of their Indian traditions into the wedding. The bride and groom exchanged floral garlands and Raj put a beautiful necklace around my Aunt's neck. When the ceremony was nearly over, I saw a woman from across the bonfire. The fire made her figure blurry and convoluted but she bore a striking resemblance to my mother. As I felt her coming closer to me, I looked back and I noticed that she had on a cardinal necklace. The cardinal was incased in a crystal heart and it stood out against her yellow dress.

After the ceremony, as I began to walk into the house, she caught up with me and put her hand on my shoulder.

"Sandra, please wait a moment," she pleaded. She had the familiar scent of lilacs about her. As I looked into her hazel eyes a feeling of peace, love and vulnerability overcame me. I knew that this was the woman I longed for, for so many years. In a voice that was as soft as an angel's whisper, she spoke to me.

"Sandra, my dearest, I am so proud of you. Please know that I will always be with you, watching over you. You will have a wonderful life. Keep our family close and God even closer. Do all the good that you can do in this world. I'm looking forward to seeing all the beautiful children that you and Johnny will have. I will see you again, dear Sandra, but it won't be for many years. Keep this necklace in remembrance of me."

She then unclipped her necklace and pressed it firmly into the palm of my hand.

"We will reunite one day in a place more wonderful than you can imagine. I must go now. I have been called to move on."

With that she kissed me on the cheek and gave me a sweet embrace. I will remember the sweet feeling of that kiss and hug as long as I live. Quickly, she walked away and began to fade away, disappearing from this world.

Suddenly my legs felt weak and my head felt light. I cried out. "Mom, wait come back!" I wasn't sure if the words I cried were audible or just in my head. Apparently, I had fainted.

The next thing that I remember is Johnny, my father, Sam, and Gran and Grandpapa all gathered around me.

My dad had woken me with smelling salts. He was calling out, "Sandra, wake up!" At the same time Johnny was stroking my forehead.

The cardinal necklace was still in the palm of my hand and I knew that seeing my mother wasn't just a dream.

Gran had a glass of water and a hand full of crackers that everyone insisted I eat. "You must make certain that you don't neglect to eat and drink regularly, dear child. Denying yourself can result in fainting or worse." Gran said.

I felt that I should keep the encounter with my mother to myself. After all, there is no need to risk sounding crazy. So, I just replied, "Yes, Gran." Then I tucked the necklace away in my pocket.

I did not mean to take away from my aunts wedding celebration. Once I was back on my feet I apologized profusely to

Raj and my now Aunt "Sunanda". Apparently, an Indian bride often changes her first name once she is married.

She assured me that it didn't have a negative effect on their celebration. She said that she was just pleased that I was alright and she remarked that the party was just getting underway.

There was food and drink, galore! They had a live band with a variety of Indian music and modern western music. Raj and Sunanda danced the first dance to Elvis's "I Can't Help Falling in Love with You". Shortly after, my father asked me to dance. Next, Johnny and his mom joined us, followed by Johnny's dad and Stacey.

It was so adorable, Sam cut in on Stacey's dad by tapping him on the shoulder. Even though they are just kids, you could see the sparks flying when Sam and Stacey were dancing together! Sam is such a little gentleman. Soon, almost everyone was dancing. We ate, drank and danced some more, all under the stars. What a beautiful romantic evening. For one night I forgot all my worries, classes, tests, and all of my responsibilities. This night was as close I have ever been to Heaven on Earth. Good night dear diary.

September 24, 1964

Johnny and I took Stacey and Sam out today. We went to the zoo. We looked at the animals but we had the most fun watching Stacey and Sam. They are so sweet together. They started holding hands by the elephants and I don't think they let go of each other all day. Although, they are too young to fall in real love (Stacey is 10 and Sam is 12), I would at least call it puppy love!

When Johnny dropped Sam and me off, Johnny gave me a sweet kiss on my cheek. I looked over at Sam and he was giving Stacey a kiss on the hand. It was so cute!

"Stacey would you do me the honor of being my guest at our farewell dinner next Saturday?" he asked.

Stacey replied, "You bet, Sam!"

CHAPTER TEN
OCTOBER

October 1, 1964

Tonight, was the farewell dinner. It was hard to say good-bye to Gran, Grandpapa, and Sam. I will miss them so and I'm not certain when I will see them again. They said that I am welcome to come any time and also that they will be in the process of moving into Uncle Harold's former estate over the next several months. After that, they said that there will be room for all of us to stay there. They suggested that we have a weeklong family reunion next summer. We all agreed that it was a wonderful idea! I hope that it comes true!

The dinner and get-together was fab. This was despite the looming melancholy of knowing that it would be our last night together for some time. We talked, ate and played Scrabble. When the fire had dimmed to a just few sparks, Grandpapa stood up and announced that it has been wonderful, but the time has come for them to leave. We all gave heartfelt hugs and kisses goodbye, with the exception of Raj and Sunanda who had volunteered to be their ride to the airport tomorrow.

I watched as Sam and Stacey said their goodbyes. They hugged each other and Sam gave Stacey a kiss on the cheek. I heard him declare that this would not be a final goodbye, but a temporary separation. He told her that he is certain that they will see each other again soon.

Well, it's back to college tomorrow for me. I have three tests this week. I hope to see you soon dear diary!

October 31, 1964

Hello dear diary, I have been incredibly busy, but life has been good. I do miss my dad, Sunanda and Raj. That is, when

I have time to miss them. Today is Halloween and dad asked me if I would come home for dinner tonight, help hand out candy, and also help him transform a pumpkin into a scary Jack o Lantern.

Johnny and I have plans to go through a haunted house with Joann and Ernie later, but I felt I should put a few hours aside to see the family. I have a feeling that they miss me as much or maybe even more than I miss them.

Raj and Sunanda picked me up at college, but dad hasn't arrived yet. So, I thought I spend a few minutes catching up with you.

As we pulled up to the house, I was amazed how much our house looks like the quintessential haunted house. Bare trees, crows flying around, and a scare crow aunt Sunanda made. Is all that needed to complete the picture is a full moon.

When I was twelve or so we only would have a few trick or treaters. It was my first year to stay home. So, I dressed up as a witch and handed out the candy. We decided that since we had so few trick or treaters, we would start giving out full size candy bars. Word got out and each year the numbers have increased. Last year we were up to fifty–three!

My grades in college have been slightly lower than they were in high school. To be honest, college classes are much more difficult. At least I am only taking three classes to start out with. Joann and I have been getting along great. Fortunately, she takes school as seriously as I do.

Well it sounds like dads' home. I hate to cut you short, but I had better go!

CHAPTER ELEVEN
THANKSGIVING

November 26, 1964

Hello dear diary,

Today was my first day home for nearly a month. It was really heartwarming to see my family again. My aunt and Raj have taken over the guest room and turned it into their own private sitting/TV/living room. They have really made it their own. It stands apart from the rest of the house with its Indian décor—ivory, ebony and wooden carvings that are displayed around the room and in bookcases with glass doors. There are lots of red and black woven cloths covering the tables. They even have incense burning that gives out a wonderful sandalwood aroma. It's so groovy! Then there's a bit of western décor. What is it you ask? Well, of course, it is a brand new 19" color television set!

Father, Johnny, Raj, Sunanda, and I had a lovely Thanksgiving Day. Sunanda and Raj did most of the cooking while Father, Johnny, and I played Scrabble and watched TV. It was the most delicious Thanksgiving feast I have ever had the pleasure of devouring. Later in the evening Johnny and I went and had pie with his family.

I have three days off and then it's back to everything college. Classes, tests, crazy college kids, and Joann. I'm so glad that I have her to room with. She is the perfect room-mate! While other kids are going to wild parties, Joann, Ernie, Johnny, and I go out on double dates. We go to dinner, for walks, to the movies and just have an all-around great time.

We all know about the drugs and drinking on campus. For the four of us, our common goal is to get through college avoiding all of that.

I feel so lucky and blessed to have these three great friends to hang out with. Who knows what kind of ways I would fall into without them!

During the week, when we are all caught up with our studies, we watch TV. There are a bunch of hilarious new sitcoms out that are a scream! Some of our favorites include "The Adams Family", "Bewitched", and "The Munsters". We laugh out loud throughout all three of these shows. Their writers are so talented!

The mansion the Adams family lives in reminds me a little of our house. Although it is a bit larger than ours. Also, our house doesn't have the creepy menagerie and all the kooky oddities.

Well, I'm not sure when I'll see you again dear diary. Perhaps over Christmas break.

CHAPTER TWELVE
CHRISTMAS BREAK

December 23, 1964

We meet again dear diary. I have to say that I am feeling displaced today. When I came home for Christmas break the other day, my room was filled with boxes. Father said that he is going to make my bedroom into a guest room and I should pack everything up. He said that he will store it for me until I have a home of my own.

I don't feel like I'm ready to give up my childhood home. I feel like my dorm room is my home away from home not a replacement home. Father assured me that I am welcome to come home anytime I would like to, especially for holidays and the summer. That was somewhat of a comfort to me although I still feel like a baby bird not quite ready to leave the nest and fly. I guess that I'm being pushed out of the nest regardless.

You, dear diary, will be safe in a very special box. I will leave you with all my "look at" dolls, my cardinal music box, and my cardinal necklace to keep you company. Farewell, dear diary. I will miss you! But I am certain that we will meet again someday.

CHAPTER THIRTEEN
MAY 2013

May 15, 2013

Well, dear diary, to say it has been too long would be quite the understatement! I found you tucked away with my "look at" dolls, cardinal necklace, and music box. It's hard to believe that it has been nearly 50 years since we have had the opportunity to chat. I have just moved from my home of 40 years. This was the home I loved. The home that my kids grew up in. The home that Johnny and I had a wonderful life in. We had by the way, three lovely daughters and one golden son.

John passed away five years ago now, and upon the relentless urging of my three daughters I have finally moved into a retirement community. I do know a few of my neighbors. Jill, across the street is the mother of my son William's childhood best friend. Down the street is my former water exercise instructor, Jan—the same Janet from my youth who ditched Joann at the World's Fair in 1964 and had a baby out of wedlock. The three of us actually became close friends over the years. Janet became a career woman—a fashion designer in New York City. She never married nor did she have any more children.

Joann married Ernie and had five children. Ernie is still with us but sadly Joann passed away five years before Johnny. She died after a long battle with colon cancer. Ernie and I have lunch occasionally and he works out at same health club that I go to. It's always a treat to see his smiling face.

Then next door is the residence of my dearest and closest friend, Sarah. Sarah was the best neighbor anyone could have wished or prayed for. Her house was across the street from ours. A developer bought up the land across from our house and built a whole new neighborhood.

Sarah, like me, had 3 daughters, and each one was born within a year of each of mine. Our girls played together all summer long from sunrise until sunset. Having the same childhood for my children that I had always wished for myself made me as satisfied as a puppy who had just dug up his long-lost bone!

It is so wonderful to have my old friend Sarah next door. Though, there is a sad part to this story. Sarah's mind seems to be declining at a faster rate than the rest of ours. It began a couple of years ago with her forgetting names. She still does remember my name, but her vision is also deteriorating. Well enough of that. Tomorrow, I will fill you in with some more details of my well-lived life!

May 16, 2013

Hello, again, Dear Diary!

I shall begin where I left off way back in nineteen-sixty-four. It was indeed a very special and formative year. As a matter of fact, as I look back, it was one of the most important years of my life. I blossomed that year. I changed from a quiet closed bud that had yet to see the sun, to a beautiful rose blooming beneath rays of sunshine. I fear now that I am sixty-eight and slightly past my prime, I maybe slowly dropping some of my precious petals.

In nineteen-sixty-four I started dating the first and last love of my life. I connected with my Aunt Sunanda and my maternal grandparents. I discovered a dear brother that I

123

never knew existed. I started college; I became an heiress. Yes, nineteen-sixty-four was quite the pivotal year!

Nineteen-sixty-five, sixty-six and sixty-seven were all good years as well. Johnny and I continued with college. Upon graduation Johnny decided that after taking a year off and working he would apply to Harvard Medical School. Well, Johnny did not need to look for work, as his job came to him.

Johnny's number was up; he was drafted! Thankfully, Johnny was placed in the Quartermaster Division. He worked in a hospital just outside of Saigon. His assignment was mainly in the records department which kept him safe, but also bored. He would often finish his assignments early and then volunteer to make blood runs. This provided him with a little more variety and action. Bringing blood to the wounded soldiers made him feel more useful. But at the same time, he was closer to harm's way. I am thankful that Johnny spared me the worry by neglecting to tell me about the blood runs in his letters. The experience left Johnny nearly deaf in one ear.

On a more cheerful note, before Johnny left, we had a grand wedding. I wore a beautiful sleeveless linen gown which is still hanging under a plastic cover in my closet. The V-neck-line and the bottom of the gown are trimmed with three-dimensional silk flowers. I wore white elbow-length gloves and, for the one and only time in my life, a hoop under my dress. This made the dress look full and added to the glamour. I had a ten-foot-long train with three girls behind me throwing flowers and caring for my train.

Johnny looked to me like the most handsome man on earth. He had on his black tuxedo with a violet colored bow tie, cummerbund and handkerchief. All of this matched the flowers on my Maid of Honor's and three bridesmaid's dresses.

We were married in the old Trinity Church. I still can picture the expression of love in Johnny's eyes as he watched me walk down the aisle with my father. It made me feel as if I was the most important, the most well-loved person in the universe. As I walked down the aisle I felt as if I were a princess preparing to take the thrown as queen.

The reception was held in my father's house in the back yard. We had a live band and danced all evening under the stars. As I look back, as it should be for every bride, it was one of the best days of my life.

After our wedding we flew to Allentown, Pennsylvania and rented a car. We drove up into the Pocono Mountains and had an unforgettable honeymoon. We stayed at a honeymoon resort and had our own private villa, complete with a round bed and a heart shaped whirlpool bathtub. Every day, we swam in the outdoor pool which was shaped like a gigantic wedding bell and basked in the sun. We ate and drank like royalty. We practiced archery, ice skated, and played tennis. Johnny and I became closer than ever. We felt as if the two of us had become one.

Nine months later our little Rebecca was born. A very beautiful, strong and healthy little girl. She had dark wavy hair and a smile that lit up my heart. But she would be eighteen months old before she would meet her father. Johnny was, of course, in Vietnam. He finally returned home and then left for a second tour six months later. Looking back, those were some of the most difficult days of my life.

Johnny's little sister, Stacey, and I became very close during those years. She helped me raise Rebecca. I paid her as a babysitter, but in reality, she was more like a co-parent. Rebecca and Stacey had the closest aunt-niece relationship I have ever seen or heard tell of. To this day they share a very special bond.

All the violence, injuries and blood and trauma that Johnny witnessed in Vietnam really had an effect on him. So much so that he decided not to go to medical school. He did however, eventually attend Harvard Law School.

There were many lean and difficult years. Sometimes I don't know how we managed to put food on the table. Despite the challenges, those years were filled with so much joy.

Two days after Rebecca's third birthday little Elizabeth was born. Elizabeth had blue eyes and blonde hair like her daddy. She was a very spirited and independent child. A year and half later Cassy (short for Cassandra and named after my mother) came along. Cassy was followed three years later by William, my little prince.

Johnny became quite successful in his law practice, and as soon as I felt the children were old enough, we embarked on a trip to the UK. We did visit other parts of Europe; however, the main event was our visit to England. We also brought Stacey with. She had turned into a beautiful young woman, with long, thick, dark, wavy hair, a slender build and an outgoing, witty and slightly flirtatious personality. She also had a smile that could melt the heart of Scrooge himself.

Secretly, I had hopes that she and Sam would get along

well. Perhaps even become more than friends. Well, dear diary, my wish was granted and then some.

Three years later Sam and Stacey became husband and wife! Every summer since then we have gone back to England to spend time with Stacey and Sam in their beautiful estate. Soon enough Sam and Stacey had a baby boy. They named him Robert after Stacey's and Johnny's mom, Roberta. Robert was soon followed by Rose. I love my little niece and nephew dearly. My children also loved their little cousins. And they are all adults now.

I grew to love and respect my mother in law Roberta even more. Surviving cancer increased her already abundant, abiding faith in the Lord. The cancer did eventually rear its ugly head again. This time though, Roberta had lived to see her children grow into wonderful, faithful successful adults and have children of their own. She handled her own death with amazing grace and dignity. She was loved by so many. She had the largest funeral I have ever seen (with the exception of my uncle Lord Harold Baden, of course.) Her wake was filled with over 600 people and flowers filled all the rooms! It was exceptionally big, considering also, that this was in 1987 prior to the days of using social media to spread the news of events!

Johnny's dad lived on and remarried a younger woman, Barbara. His wife is still alive and she lives with her daughter in Ohio. I believe she is in her early 80s now. Johnny's dad passed away in his early seventies. Thankfully it was before Johnny fell ill and passed away. As difficult as it may be to have your parent pass away, I can only imagine the horror of having your child pass away before you. Johnny never cared for Barbara much. I guess the feeling of having your mother replaced, no matter how old you are, is a difficult one to deal with.

Thankfully for me, but sadly for my father, I never had to face that situation. Dad is still with us, but I'm certain that part of him would prefer to be with my mother. He is 95 now and lives in a posh assisted living apartment just a couple of miles down the road. He is one of the few relatively healthy men living there and he is fawned on by all the elderly ladies. The main highlight of his later years has been his grandson William. All of my girls are close to Dad but nothing compares to the marvelous bond between William and his grandfather. They are so much alike; I have never seen anything like it. I think that when William was a boy, he and Dad could have happily spent twenty-four hours a day with each other. My father enjoyed Will so much, and Will has learned so much from my father.

Will now has a wife and two boys of his own, Zac and Kyle. He seems to be leading a full and happy life in Connecticut. Zac is a fine boy, nearly perfect, just like his dad. Kyle has a bit of a mischievous streak. Will brings his boys to visit four or five times a year and Dad and I try to travel to see him at least twice a year. William is a history professor. He has also published five books and many papers.

Rebecca lives within twenty minutes of me. She is a middle school librarian and has been married for twenty years. She has two beautiful daughters. My first grandchild (and just between you and me dear diary, my favorite), is Grace. She is already a senior in high school. Her youngest is Angela who is a brilliant and a very spirited child just like her Aunt

Elizabeth. Angela is just finishing up her last year of middle school.

Elizabeth (I like to call her Lizzy) is forty-one now.

She had rocky times early in life, literally! She sang in a rock band. She got mixed up with the wrong man and she had a baby boy (Joey) out of wedlock. One day Lizzy had been drinking with her boyfriend Frank. Frank demanded that Lizzy go to the store immediately to buy him a pack of cigarettes. She argued with Frank and told him that she did not want to drink and drive. Frank slapped her and threatened her with his fist. He screamed at her and chased her out of the door. While hurriedly backing her car out of the driveway she felt a thud and a bump. To her horror she had run over Joey, who was just shy of three-years-old.

An ambulance was called and Joey was rushed into surgery. Lizzy phoned me in hysterics. I rushed over to the hospital and I arrived just before the surgery was over. The surgeon came out and told us that although little Joey had made it through surgery, within minutes he will be gone. He told us that we should say our final goodbyes now. Lizzy was so brave, even as she felt the life of her little son leave his body, she asked the nurse if she could donate his organs. I was so proud of Lizzy. Now, five children live because of Joey's death.

Elizabeth faced vehicular manslaughter charges. John and I hired the best attorney available and her charges were dropped.

Elizabeth then left Frank and moved to LA. She did some modeling and she was also in some low budget horror films.

She was a mess, riddled with so much sorrow and guilt that she nearly drowned in her own tears. She developed a serious drug and alcohol problem.

Then, one Christmas Eve, I believe there was divine intervention. Lizzy was home for the holidays and we were attending the Christmas Eve service. A young man that Lizzy knew from high school choir sat next to her. While the church sang "Joy to the World" and "O Come All Ye Faithful", you could hear their marvelous voices together. They seemed to be soaring to heaven in unison above all the rest.

They chatted after the service and I'm certain that everyone there could notice the obvious chemistry between the two. The choir director approached them and talked them into a singing a duet at the next Sunday service. Chills crept up and down my spine as I listened to their spectacular voices resounding together in worship. My heart nearly leapt right out of my chest. Johnny and I grinned knowingly at each other. He held my hand. We both realized at that very moment that they were meant to be together.

Lizzy and Michael started dating shorty after that. They have been happily married for ten years now. They have a little girl so sweet that she could melt an iceberg into the ocean. Brielle, just turned seven. They also have a baby boy on the way.

Cassy, my youngest girl is thirty-nine. Cassy would move mountains to please me. In high school she was a straight A student. She attended Wharton Business College and got her MBA. She had a wonderful career in New York City and met the man of her dreams, Mike. Mike was a powerful executive and worked in the Twin Towers. He died on 9-11, a hero saving others, and many grateful souls have told stories of how he helped them exit the building quickly and safely. Cassy told me that she received a phone call from Aunt Sunanda just before Mike left for work that morning. Aunt Sunanda told her that Mike should stay home. She couldn't give a concrete reason and being the dedicated career man that Mike was, he ignored the warning and went to work anyway.

Cassy has moved back to Boston now where she has opened her own successful flower shop. She has wonderful business and people skills. I see her at least once a week. My hope is that she will find love in time to have children of her own.

Cassy loves to run. She ran cross country in high school and college. Just last month she was going to participate in the Boston Marathon, but as she was about to walk out the door, the phone rang. It was Aunt Sunanda pleading with her to stay home. Thank you, Aunt Sunanda and thank God that Cassy listened! There was a bombing that day, near the finish line of the Marathon. Three people were killed and hundreds of others were injured.

Three days later Aunt Sunanda's heart gave out. Raj was by her side. Outwardly, he did not remember her name. But even though he was suffering from Alzheimer's he held one hand and I the other as she left this world. There was a nurse present who quietly told me that she didn't have long but that she could still hear me. Hearing, she said, was the last sense to leave us.

As I held her hand, I spoke with her, thanking her for all she did for me, reminding her of the precious moments that we shared from the first time that she comforted me and I realized that she was wasn't scary and heartless after all, all the way through the time she saved Cassy's life. I tried to hold back the tears, but as I spoke, my throat swelled up and tears streamed down my face. Finally, I told her that I believe I will see her in heaven one day. Within moments I felt the life leave her body, and as I sobbed her hand became limp and the warmth in her hand cooled.

The most heart-breaking part of her death was Raj's reaction. He called her name again and again. I told him that she was gone. He replied in shock, "What do you mean GONE?" He shook her over and over again, crying out, "What's happening?" Finally, the staff medicated him and he fell asleep.

There was a sickness in the pit of my stomach as I left. I felt as if I could vomit at any moment. As soon as I arrived home, I began to pray that God would take care of Raj and minimize his pain.

Five hours later, I received a call from the care facility that they resided in. Raj had left this world also.

Dearest Diary, I believe that now I have brought you up to date with everyone. I will say farewell…

CHAPTER FOURTEEN
APRIL 2019

April 22, 2019

Dear diary, I apologize for the nearly six-year delay in writing. I have been living a full and happy life. My father passed away in 2014. His heart failed him. My children have all been thriving as have my grandchildren. Elizabeth's second baby boy was born. A very cheerful and sweet boy with Down syndrome.

I really live for the large family holidays. I am so pleased that I can share them with my children, grandchildren, son, daughters, and daughter-in-law, something I missed so much as I was growing up. I now have nine grandchildren, three daughters, three son-in-law's, and one very special son and daughter-in-law. I do have to share some holidays with the other grandparents but this Christmas day all of us were together at my house. Everyone was here for Easter, too.

There is a compelling reason that I am choosing to write now. My health has been failing the last few months. I am finding physical activity to be more and more difficult. Two weeks ago, it was a struggle just to make it out to the mail box. Today, I could barely make it to the bathroom. I fear that my heart will give out soon. Do not mourn for me as I can't imagine anyone having a more full and wonderful life. Also, I'm sure that the next world, the one God has promised us, will be even better.

I have been reminiscing lately. Recalling all the special moments in my life. Of all these moments, the one that stands out the most is surprisingly not my wedding, not the birth of my children, not saying goodbye to loved ones as they passed on, but flying over the Atlantic, frozen in time, on the verge of adulthood. Securely seated in between the man of my past and the man of my future. I hope that when I pass on, I will be thinking of this moment and I will pass with an ever so slight grin on my lips.

April 23, 2019

This morning dear diary, I had a divine encounter. On my window sill, there appeared our friend the cardinal. I gathered up all my strength and walked over to the window. When I attempted to open the window, it didn't stick and require all my strength as it usually does. Instead it slid open easily, like a knife cutting soft butter. As I opened the window the cardinal flew away. Within seconds a vision of my mother appeared. She had on a flowing pale pink gown and she had large feathered, white wings. Her face was so very warm and welcoming almost as if I had seen her each and every day of my life. She held out her hands with her palms stretched out and open towards me.

Then, in her soft loving voice she spoke. "Don't be afraid, Sandra, its time. Take my hand and come with me."

I cried out, "No not yet! I'm not ready!" She then faded away.

Some may think that I am just an old woman having hallucinations or daydreams, but I know, dear diary, that you will believe me. So, we will keep it just between the two of us. I must lay down now. Goodbye, dear diary, you have been a wonderful friend to me.

EPILOGUE

Dear readers:

I am Sandra's eldest daughter Rebecca. I learned from my mother's diary that it was a dream of hers to become a published author someday. Even though she didn't fulfill that dream in her lifetime my hope is that she will know that it is fulfilled now. I found this diary in her bed-side drawer and I couldn't think of a better way to honor her life then to have this published.

My mother passed away the day after her last entry. She had called me and told me she knew that she didn't have long and that she would like me to gather the family as soon as possible. We were all with her for hours saying our goodbyes. When we left to go out to dinner, she had a look of complete serenity on her face. As I looked back at her, a warm glow seemed to surround her and an unusual heart shaped cardinal necklace she had around her neck was lit up and sparkling brightly.

When we came back from dinner she had passed on. She had an ever so slight little grin frozen on her face.

I believe that my mother knows and is pleased with the decision to publish her diary. As I walked out of my publisher's office, there perched on a tree was a cardinal. Its red color was amazingly vibrant. As it sang out it swooped down and landed on my shoulder. It pushed its open beak into my check as if to give me a kiss. An overwhelming sense of comfort and warmth filled me. The cardinal then flew back up to the tree branch. As I stared at it our eyes met. It captivated me. It was as if I were under a spell. After a few moments the cardinal flew up to a higher branch.

As started to walk away, the bird began chirping boisterously. The cardinal definitely had a message for me. As I continued down the path towards my car its song faded into the distance. Was this cardinal the spirit of my mother? In my heart of hearts, I believe that it was! I have a comforting feeling that my mother will be watching over me, my brother and sisters until the time comes for us to join her.

ABOUT THE AUTHOR

Roberta Quam is a passionate storyteller and a 20th century history buff. She is a child of the 1960s. Roberta is the daughter of an internationally renowned biochemistry professor and a British war bride who delighted in entertaining her husband's diverse colleagues from abroad. Roberta's mother travelled the world at her husband's side. She regaled in telling her three daughter's tales of her past life in England. Roberta grew up in Minnesota. This was sharply contrasted by spending many childhood vacations in England. Following college Roberta moved back to her hometown, married and had two children. After years of traveling, working in varied fields and being a homemaker, she finally has the opportunity to pursue her dream of becoming a published author.

Made in the USA
Coppell, TX
29 April 2021